FALLEN ANGEL

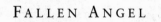

Also by Don J. Snyder

NIGHT CROSSING

OF TIME AND MEMORY: MY PARENTS' LOVE STORY

THE CLIFF WALK

FROM THE POINT

A SOLDIER'S DISGRACE

VETERANS PARK

FALLEN ANGEL

A Novel

DON J. SNYDER

POCKET BOOKS

NEW YORK LONDON TORONTO SYDNEY SINGAPORE

POCKET BOOKS, a division of Simon & Schuster, Inc.
1230 Avenue of the Americas, New York, NY 10020

Library of Congress Cataloging-in-Publication Data

Snyder, Don J.
    Fallen angel: a novel / Don J. Snyder.
       p. cm.
    ISBN 0-7434-2231-7
    1. Fathers—Death—Fiction. 2. First loves—Fiction. 3. Maine—Fiction.
I. Title.

    PS3569.N86 F35 2001
    813'.54—dc21

                                                                2001041431

First Pocket Books hardcover printing October 2001

10 9 8 7 6 5 4 3 2 1

POCKET and colophon are registered trademarks of
Simon & Schuster, Inc.

For information regarding special discounts for bulk purchases, please
contact Simon & Schuster Special Sales at 1-800-456-6798
or business@simonandschuster.com

Designed by C. Linda Dingler

Printed in the U.S.A.

*To Cecilia, who blessed our
lives with her presence*

FALLEN ANGEL

PROLOGUE

This is always with me now. The way I saw her that first morning as she came up from the shore, across the ice-glazed granite rocks that stood at the opening of the harbor. A long blue denim dress. Dark hair, black as ink, in a thick braid lying across her left shoulder. She was holding the hand of a small child in a green cloth coat. They were both wearing silly red puddle boots, so inappropriate for a winter day in Maine. There was a yellow dog running out ahead of them. Or was it later, at the cottage, where I first saw the dog?

This is the difficulty I am up against, trying to recall her precisely as I first saw her in those beginning moments, just the plain and exquisite portrait of her when she was still a stranger to me. Her shape, a few brush strokes out-lined against the bruised, winter sky behind her, before I knew the thousand things I would come to learn about her. When I acknowledge my life before I knew her, when I go back and stand alone in the emptiness before she entered my life, I see that I was a blind man. Blind to the mystery that surrounds us. Blind to the holiness of this world, to the way the wind collects our voices then scatters them across the open fields of memory and time. Maybe you were standing beside me that first morning in the ordinary light of the vanishing stars, when she was still distinct and separate from the story she gave to me, and I am giving to you now. A story which began in the last moment of her absence, before I felt the weight of her first touch.

There is a deep loneliness in life that can take our breath away and leave us weary. I saw the loneliness in her and could tell that she had come a long way to that shore in Maine. Didn't I see her weariness right away that morning? The way her shoulders were pitched forward slightly in her blue coat. She would tell me that this was a real navy peacoat, a relic from the 1960s when such coats were the fashion of the young people's army and not some expensive late-twentieth-century version from the Gap. Before she turned and walked away down the snow-covered lane, still holding the child's hand, she leaned against a fence post and bowed her head and I was struck by her weariness, surprised, the way you would be surprised to find the shoes of a department store mannequin worn through on the soles.

But beyond that, what could a blind man have known then? That we are made whole by our fears and desires? That the passage of time is indifferent to our dreams? If you were standing there would you have seen that she and I, in our separate ways, held the broken ends of an old story, and that we had come together in those cold winter days in Maine, drawn out from our dark history, free to finally join the broken ends together?

1

I suppose our lives are nothing more than a collection of moments. Some moments tell us who we are. Others, what we've run away from. I was eight years old the year our story began, just a boy, but I can place its beginning in the moment my father came to pick me up from Mrs. Fisher's third-grade class. I looked up from my desk and there he was, standing in the doorway of the classroom in his royal blue carpenter's overalls that zipped up from the knees to his chin. Because I had never seen my father in my school before, something about his presence was a little unbelievable. And when other parents began lining up behind him in the doorway I felt the same kind of confusion you feel coming out of a matinee movie, stepping into darkness where there had been light.

The school was calling parents to come collect their kids that morning. My mother must have taken the call and then reached my father over the two-way radio in his pickup truck or the telephone in his shop.

I was holding his hand. His boots, I remember, were caked with mud and we were leaving a trail along the glassy corridor. When we passed the principal's office she was standing at her window with her head bowed, crying. I remember her shoulders were shaking, and I was still thinking about this when my father lifted me into his truck and said, "The president's been shot, Terry, everybody's going home."

For the next week we ate supper in the living room on TV trays, watching the evening news. In those days my father kept some of his carpenter's tools in a honey-colored wood chest in the kitchen next to the copper boiler. The chest was a perfect cube, three feet long by three feet wide by three feet deep, with little trapdoors and secret compartments and folding shelves. Lift the lid and you found a crosscut saw and a coping saw fastened by bronzed wing nuts to the other side. A bevel with a mahogany handle in a vertical drawer. A set of flat files lined up by ascending heights. That week when there was so much sadness and my mother kept crying in front of the TV in her curlers, I daydreamed of being inside my father's tool chest, stretching out my legs against a bronze level, resting my head in the smooth, curved hemlock handle of a block plane.

You remember the picture on television that November of John John saluting his father's casket? I think that picture was the reason my father began taking me to work with him on the days I wasn't in school. He'd never taken me with him before, and I came to believe that the young president's death had cut him open and that my father's way of coping was to pull me closer to him.

Our work mornings began with me pushing a stool from the kitchen table up to the counter so I could turn on the weather radio while my father did his push-ups on the floor. All his life he wore a Saint Christopher medallion on a silver chain around his neck, and with each push-up, it clinked against the linoleum.

On the way to work we stopped at Bridie's Hardware in Oak Hill for whatever supplies my father needed. There was a calendar with ladies in bathing suits above the cash register. We would load our supplies into the back of the truck and it would still be dark when we drove down to the end of the Blackpoint Road where the town of Ellsworth turned into Rose Point. There was an electric gate my father opened with a key, and beyond the gate a world you couldn't really believe even when you were there, looking at it. A high promontory of open fields and meadows set just back from the ocean, surrounded by giant fir trees, lime-colored bluffs that looked out over a milelong strand of beach, and twenty-two cottages hidden along narrow gravel lanes. Designed by the famous Indiana architect Leslie Woodhead, and built at the turn of the century by Pennsylvania steel and oil barons, these cottages were mansions really, sprawling four-story places, stick-framed and cedar-shingled, with turrets and

gabled roofs and screened sleeping porches that faced the
sea.

It was one of Maine's private colonies, a summer place
that was abandoned to the care of my father during the off
season. He had keys to each house, and the owners
employed him to repair the damage done by the fierce
storms that battered Rose Point all winter. In a shed beside
the thirteenth green of the golf course he had a small wood
shop where he kept his tools, a three-horsepower table
saw, a planer, miter saw, belt sander, drill press, and, in a
set of pigeonhole boxes salvaged from the old summer
post office when it was remodeled, he kept the keys to
each camp under a named slot; this was one rule of Rose
Point, that each proprietor name his camp and print this
name in discrete black letters on a rectangle oak board
that my father spar varnished every spring and hung from
the front-porch eaves.

Northwinds. The Ark. Fair Haven. Kettle Cove. I suppose the idea was that a name on your house could make
you feel less temporary about yourself.

I went inside all the camps with my father that winter.
In *Long Rest* there was a photograph of the owner standing beside President Eisenhower. The chandeliers and
bronze light fixtures in *Homeward* came from the Spanish
ocean liner *Queen Isadora,* when she was decommis-
sioned at the turn of the century. On the marble-floored
foyer of *Last Light,* Clark Gable once greeted evening

guests. An electronic panel of bells that summoned maids and butlers was still in working order there. In *Maine Stay* my father once filled all five claw-footed bathtubs with bottles of champagne and ice before a party. The backyard of *Right Way* had been transformed into a fantastic minia-ture replica of Yankee Stadium, with every detail, includ-ing the dugouts and outfield walls, built to scale. For twenty-nine years my father cut the infield grass wearing soft leather slippers and using a push mower whose wheels he had covered with felt.

From Memorial Day until Columbus weekend the lanes at Rose Point were swarming with summer people from far away. Sailing was their main activity; each camp had a boat, and regattas were held four times a week. Following an old tradition, the skippers sailed in dark blue double-breasted coats with gold buttons and striped ties. Evening lectures were held in the stone library, picnic lunches at the beach house, and book fairs with Punch and Judy puppet shows on the library lawn.

After Columbus Day weekend my father locked up the camps for the long winter. He drained the pipes and shut off the electricity and capped the chimneys. He covered the furniture in white sheets. And then, in the spring, these chores were reversed. Putting the cottages to bed and then waking them up was how my father described this. He preferred the winter, when he had free run of the point and could come and go like a proprietor. When the summer people were there, he was just hired help and he had to use the servants' entrances and do his work without being seen or heard.

That winter of 1963, two weeks before Christmas, my father got word that he was to open the *Serenity* cottage. He told my mother and me about it at dinner one night.

"Backward," he said. "No heat. Pipes will freeze. Rich people are silly sometimes."

"Not only rich people," my mother reminded him.

He didn't acknowledge her. "But, if they want me to open the place, I'll open it."

The next morning at the hardware store I listened to my father telling old Mr. Bridie what he was up against.

"Who do these people think they are, anyway?" Bridie wanted to know.

"Yeah, well, there it is," my father said.

"Don't they know it's winter up here?"

"I wonder," my father said. Whenever he spoke of the people he worked for it was with a kind of solemn resignation.

"*Summer people,*" Mr. Bridie growled. "They're supposed to migrate with the birds. We shouldn't have to deal with them again until June."

My father was a man who hurried through life, leaving behind him the doubters of the world, the cautious and the circumspect. He was the only man I ever knew to wrap his legs outside the rungs of ladders and slide down full speed, stopping himself just before he hit the ground. And so I have remembered clearly how we entered the cottage without making a sound, my father *so careful,* using both hands to ease the door closed behind us. We followed the shaft of yellow light from his flashlight and walked slowly from room to room. Slowly and silently, with reverence, the way you would walk through an empty church. This made me wonder in my child's imagination if another life went on inside the empty cottages through the dark winters. If people moved in secretly after the summer people left. *They were living here in* Serenity. *They had heard us coming and they were hiding, watching us.*

Inside the cottage it was as dark and cold as a cave. Through the cracks of doorways and around windowsills snow as fine as grains of sugar had blown inside and lay in small white drifts. A pyramid of snow on the counter beside a toaster. A carpet of snow in the alcove. In the library, my father ran his hand along the spines of a row of books, centering them on the shelf. He stepped back from a painting in the dining room to make sure that it was straight on the wall. Because he never took even a passing interest in the appointments of his own house, where he often tracked a trail of mud and sawdust, the time I spent with my father at Rose Point taught me that a certain dignity attends the work we do to earn our living.

It took two days to fill every room with light. There were more than seventy windows and doors, each covered with a sheet of plywood, fastened with screws in all four corners. My father had to climb a ladder to reach the windows on the second and third floors. I stood at the bottom, holding the ladder for him and watching the soles of his boots move up and down above my head. It was so cold we had to stop every hour and sit in my father's truck with the heater roaring. After we finished the last window and went back inside and stood in the lighted rooms, it was as if music had been turned on inside the cottage.

What I remember best about those days opening up *Serenity* is my father setting the mousetraps and letting me bait them with little bits of cheese. You had to be careful not to get your fingers caught. We put traps in cupboards, under beds, and in the medicine cabinets in the bathrooms. We set them all and then when it got dark in the late afternoon, before we headed home, we sat on the first-floor landing, my father with a finger to his lips. "Listen," he whispered. There was the sound of the wind rattling the windows and racing down the chimneys and then, gradually, the snapping of the traps like firecrackers. One, then silence, then another. Like most children I had learned from my storybooks to assign human emotions to animals, and those nights, lying in bed, all I could think about was some mother mouse and her babies waiting hopelessly for the father mouse to make it home with cheese for dinner.

Because the cottages were so close to the ocean none of them had basements. Beneath *Serenity* there was a crawl space in the dirt. I held the flashlight for my father while he dragged in bales of hay to insulate the water pipes. He built a box around the water pump and wired a lightbulb inside it to keep the pump from freezing.

On the fourth or fifth day we made one last trip to Bridie's store after the owner of *Serenity* had called my father, instructing him to build a skating rink in the front yard. "That takes the cake, Paul, if you ask me," Bridie said to my father.

We bought a canvas tarp and put the plow on my father's truck to clear away a square in the deep snow. We laid the tarp down in the square and hammered two-by-sixes into the frozen ground around the border. That night my father hooked up a hose and let water trickle onto the canvas. By morning the ice was an inch thick and smooth as glass. Years later I learned that the owner of the cottage had been an All-American hockey player at Harvard and captain of the United States Olympic team that competed in Innsbruck, Austria.

The last thing we did in the cottage before the owner arrived with his family was bring in Christmas trees for the three living rooms and the library on the first floor and one for the glassed-in widow's walk on the ridge of the roof. This one we decorated with colored lights. The moment we plugged it in, a stillness fell over us. I saw a look of surprise on my father's face. In later years whenever I recalled that moment, I thought of it as a look of wonder, the way an artist might gaze upon a finished painting that turned out to be more beautiful than anything he ever believed he could paint. My father turned me toward the glass windows and pointed to the black ocean. He told me that there were ships out there in the darkness and men onboard who would see the lighted tree. "You never know, son," he said, "this may help some poor soul find his way home."

2

Three days before Christmas, a northeaster began tracking across the North Atlantic, on gale force winds from Nova Scotia, that drove temperatures along the Maine coast to twenty-five below zero. The ice was so thick in the harbor you could walk across the channel to Dutton's lighthouse. My father worked forty-eight-hour shifts helping lobstermen haul their boats out of the cove before their wooden hulls were crushed. The storm tide and ice on the morning of the twenty-third snapped the cedar underpinnings beneath Penny's clam shack on the pier, and breaking waves ripped out all the oceanside windows and doors on the Fish and Game office on the wharf.

Out at sea the crew of an oil tanker sailing from Finland had to be rescued by the Coast Guard after the ship was blown off course and ran aground.

While the storm advanced, my mother and I kept a fire going in the living room and sat by the two-way radio waiting for word from my father, who called in periodically to tell us when he expected to return home to refill his thermos with black coffee that my mother laced with apricot brandy to help keep him warm.

When the Maine turnpike was closed to traffic late in the afternoon of the twenty-third, my father said he was sure that the Halworths wouldn't be able to make the trip, and that all our work at the *Serenity* cottage had been for nothing. But on Christmas Eve morning word came that Mr. Halworth had hired a man with a truck and a plow in Kittery for an escort, and they were driving up Old Route 1 through the storm. I remember my father standing in his long johns, staring out the window at the blowing snow after he hung up the telephone. My mother and I were drying the felt liners of his boots on the woodstove. "Someone should tell them to turn back," my mother said. "Don't they have a child with them?"

"How do you tell a rich man he can't do something," my father said. "You know these people."

He had dressed and put on his coat and was in the foyer ready to go to the point when he stopped and asked me if I wanted to come along with him.

"You'll be careful?" my mother said.

He opened the front door and didn't look back.

It took us over an hour to drive seven miles. Every few minutes the windshield wipers iced up and my father had to climb out of the truck and clean them off. At the end of the Broad Turn Road he rolled down his window and pointed to the Rose Point Yacht Club. "Watch this, Terry," he said. "You may never see this again in your lifetime."

Through the blowing snow, the dock and the buildings looked like nothing real, nothing more than dark shadows standing against the white sky. Then a darker shadow appeared behind the buildings, and with it a dull thundering as a giant wave rose from the sea or fell from the sky over the roof tops of the yacht club and the outbuildings. It seemed as if the earth had been tilted to one side. The breaking wave crashed over the jetty, roared up the side of the hill, and washed across the road. I could feel our truck rocking from side to side as seawater took hold of the tires. "A wave like that," my father proclaimed, "could have come all the way from Africa."

After we passed through the electric gate at the entrance to the point my father told me to move closer to him. We dropped our plow and he held me back against the seat as he gunned the engine. All the way down Winslow Homer Lane the tall cedar trees were bending low in the wind, and the mansions kept appearing and then dissolving away to nothing in the blowing snow.

At *Serenity* cottage we plowed the driveway open, and then shoveled a path to the front porch. We found the nearest wood pile and carried logs and kindling onto the porch, stacking it beneath a lean-to my father made out of two shutters to keep the firewood dry.

Inside we turned on all the lights and laid in newspaper, kindling, and logs in all seven fireplaces. I remember opening the refrigerator and being shocked to find its shelves stocked with food. My father was a man who always waited in his truck in the parking lot of the IGA when my mother went grocery shopping. He'd always claimed that the displays of food made him dizzy. I couldn't imagine how he had known what to buy for a family he knew so little about.

We were halfway down the Winslow Homer road heading home when my father remembered one more thing he wanted to do.

He found his way to the skating rink he had built along one side of the cottage, next to the gazebo, and plowed off the snow, our headlights reflecting off the ice and our tires sliding sideways.

Shortly before noon we returned home. There was nothing to do then but eat our lunch and wait for the Halworths to arrive.

I was watching *Lassie* on television when Sheriff Kane came by in his cruiser with Christmas presents for us, a bottle of scotch for my father, a box of chocolates for my mother, and for me a small box that my father told me to put under the tree and open on Christmas morning. The year before, Sheriff Kane had presented me with a real deputy badge, and I was dying to see what he'd bought me this year. "Let him open it now," my mother said. "Sure, why not?" the sheriff agreed.

It was a container about the size of a cigarette box. One half held an ink pad and little sheets of onion skin paper. The other side, white powder and a small brush. The sheriff waited until I figured it out.

"A fingerprinting set," I said.

He knew how pleased I was. "That's no toy, Terry," he said to me as I was examining it. "That's the real McCoy, the same little number that my deputies and me keep at the station."

I was so thrilled with it that I brought it with me when my father and I returned to the *Serenity* cottage late in the day, and Charles Halworth, a tall man with wide shoulders and black hair, made a big deal out of it when he saw it in my hand. "Well, that *is* something," he said. There was a kind of melody in his voice that matched the quick, graceful way he moved. He had his daughter on his shoulders when he knelt down in front of me and held his hand out. "Do me the honors, won't you?" he said. I looked at my father, who stood off a ways with his hat in his hand. Then I took Mr. Halworth's fingerprint while his daughter looked down silently at me from her perch on her father's shoulders.

"Thanks," he said, giving me his other hand to shake. "Now if I ever get lost you'll be able to track me down."

I was drawn to the man the way children are always drawn to those rare adults who do not condescend to them and who seem to understand precisely how boring the world of grown-ups is.

His wife, on the other hand, was busy in the kitchen and didn't pay any attention to me or my father.

"Say, here's the reason I called you over," Mr. Halworth said to my father as he led us upstairs. In the bedroom with the telescope he told my father that his wife had lost a diamond earring two summers before in the cracks between the wide pine floorboards. "All the way up this morning I had a feeling I was going to find it, and the minute I stepped into the room—bingo!" he said enthusiastically. "See, look right down here."

He needed my father to pry up a board so he could retrieve it.

My father went to his truck to get a hammer. While he worked on the floorboard I knelt beside him, and we looked at each other when we heard Mrs. Halworth raising her voice about something in another room. "Not *that* again," I heard her say. A door was slammed a moment later and the cottage seemed to fill with a sadness that remained even after Mr. Halworth appeared in the doorway dressed in a Santa Claus outfit.

I was so surprised that what happened next seemed oddly disconnected from me. There was my father handing Mr. Halworth the diamond earring. And Mr. Halworth telling us how he had a tradition of making an appearance as Santa Claus in the children's hospital near their winter home every Christmas Eve. And Mrs. Halworth commenting that her husband had spent most of his adult life apologizing for being wealthy. And my father agreeing to let me ride to the Maine Medical Center in Portland with Mr. Halworth and his daughter. In this regard my father was reluctant.

"I'll bring him home straight away," Mr. Halworth declared.

I saw him place some money in my father's hand, though my father tried to conceal it from me.

3

Then we were riding through the snowstorm in Mr. Halworth's big Cadillac. Me in the backseat with his daughter, too scared to speak.

"The kids will love the fingerprinting kit," Mr. Halworth said above the radio, which he'd tuned to a loud rendition of "Hark the Herald Angels Sing."

He knew of a toy store in Cape Elizabeth where everything was made by hand. We spent almost an hour there, going up and down the aisles with shopping baskets and store clerks helping us. "Two of those!" he exclaimed. "Three of these!"

So much snow had fallen by the time we reached the city that half the streets were closed and it was like driving through a maze to find our way to the hospital. At one intersection a car had slammed into a telephone pole.

Mr. Halworth rolled down his window and his face grew tense as we passed the wrecked car.

"I'll get us home in just a few minutes," he said, as if he was reassuring himself.

By the time we parked and walked to the front doors of

the hospital he had recovered his excitement. He practically danced by the security guards at the main entrance, the elderly woman at the information desk, the janitors in the corridors, and the nurses at their station.

In the children's cancer ward he decorated the kids' noses with whipped cream while his daughter and I passed out gifts. In one room, where the children were too sick to get out of bed, he knelt down beside each of them and whispered something. He gave a kite to a boy whose face was as white as paper. And ballet shoes to a girl with a swollen head and a rubber hose running from one ear.

When we left, nurses and patients were dancing in our wake. Even after the elevator doors closed I could hear them calling "Merry Christmas" to us.

While we were inside the hospital the snow had changed to sleet, coating the streets and the car's windshield with ice. The defroster was blowing at top speed when we pulled out of the parking lot onto a main road. "Homeward bound," Mr. Halworth said, reaching over the seat and patting his daughter's knee. "You look like a young man who knows how to ice-skate. Am I right?" he asked me.

"I've never skated," I replied.

"Never skated? What do you think of that, Katie?" he exclaimed, turning to smile at his daughter. She smiled back at him, glanced at me, then quickly turned away.

"Tomorrow Katie and I are going to get you up on skates," Mr. Halworth said.

It was dark by now. You could barely see anything out the car windows. When we turned onto State Street, which was a steep hill running all the way to the entrance to the highway, Mr. Halworth rolled his window down again and stuck his head out to see what was ahead of us. I could see the lighted sign of the Acme supermarket through his open window, and it was only after the sign began spinning that I realized we were going sideways down the hill. "Oh God," I heard Mr. Halworth exclaim. He began pumping the brake pedal as we picked up speed. He was hunched over the dashboard, stomping harder on the brake, when a mailbox crashed through the window next to his daughter. She screamed and he jerked the steering wheel hard to the right, and then the left. A second later we hit something and his arms flew up in the air. There was a jangling sound, like we were dragging a chain, just before we crashed into a snowbank.

We had barely stopped moving when Mr. Halworth threw open his door and jumped out of the car. For an instant he stood perfectly still, and then, without looking back at us or closing his door, he ran past the front of the car. I looked over the seat and saw him drop down to his knees as if something had knocked him off his feet. I could see only the top of his red Santa Claus hat, which suddenly seemed silly and worthy of Mrs. Halworth's scorn.

I remember trying not to be afraid and not daring to look at Katherine for fear that I might find she was crying. I looked down at the floor beneath my feet, which was dark except for a narrow band of light that fell through the open car door.

When I looked up again, Mr. Halworth's red cap was gone. There was no sign of him. I wondered if his daughter had watched him disappear and I turned to look at her. Her eyes were wide open and her head was bowed. I looked away. Then back. It took a little time for me to see that she was staring at her shoes. They were shiny shoes, reflecting a streetlight behind us, and she was holding them up off the floor, staring hard at them. I looked myself and saw at once that one of her shoes had slipped off her heel and was balancing from her toes. She was trying not to move her foot. I looked into her eyes again and saw how determined she was to keep the shoe from falling off. As if we were from different parts of the world and shared no common language, we sat in silence.

In minutes there were police cars and an ambulance with their lights flashing. Except for a fireman who stuck his head inside the car and looked too surprised to say anything, no one paid any attention to us. We sat there long enough for me to begin to feel responsible for her. At last I moved close enough to her to reach down and slide the shoe back on her foot. Her heel was cold in the palm of my hand.

❦

Eventually Sheriff Kane took us to his cruiser and told us that he was going to drive us home. "Where's my daddy?" Katherine asked him.

"He'll be home soon," the sheriff told her.

I didn't know that we had hit someone until it came over Sheriff Kane's radio.

When we pulled up to the cottage, Mrs. Halworth was standing on the front porch in a long fur coat. My father's truck was parked at the end of the driveway and the light went on inside when he opened the door. He called me over and I got in. He started the truck as soon as the sheriff led the girl and her mother inside the cottage.

My father backed out into the lane. I wanted in the worst way to stay there. I didn't know why; I just wanted to stay until Mr. Halworth came back.

Though I had been riding in the car, I was one of the last people in town to learn what had happened. "It's one of those things," my father said to me when he explained that Mr. Halworth's car had struck and killed a woman and her baby. "An accident. No one is to blame."

It was my mother who finally told me that Mr. Halworth had disappeared. "He's probably still in shock. They'll find him," she said.

Christmas day the city newspaper reported the details on the front page. My father had been wrong; the woman's baby was still alive, in a coma at the Catholic hospital where the chaplain had begun a prayer vigil. For several days there were reports on television of the baby's condition and of prayer groups organized across the city. This was all everyone was talking about in our town; it seemed to capture people just as the president's assassination had. Special masses and candlelight services were held, and I remember a newspaper photograph of a group of firemen carrying bouquets of flowers into the hospital.

I was in my bedroom, dressing for school on the first day back after vacation, when my father drove all the way home from his shop to tell me he didn't want me saying anything about the accident to the kids at school. "It's better that way. Do you understand?"

I told him I did, but I didn't. "What's going to happen to the man?" I asked him.

"Nothing," he said.

"But where is he now?" I asked, hoping the way a child hopes that he was back with his daughter and her mother.

"He turned himself in," my father said. "There are no charges against him. He's not in any trouble."

So he *had* come back, just as my mother had said he would. This gave me reason to believe that everything would turn out all right.

The baby lived another week. In the newspaper there were pictures of the funeral, too sad to look at really. And then more sad news that winter when my father told us that there was going to be a divorce between Mr. and Mrs. Halworth and that Mrs. Halworth had sent a crew of men to clean out everything in the *Serenity* cottage.

Though I was only eight years old, I had a sense that my father was embarrassed by the fact that I'd been a part of the accident. He never came right out and said anything, but it was between us, and I think my mother felt it too. Maybe he imagined that my part in this tragedy would drag his name into Rose Point cocktail party conversations about the accident for years to come and he would be forever branded by the summer people who employed him.

It was spring and the story had faded away by the time I had the chance to see the cottage again. My father was working down the lane at another place, putting in underground hoses for a sprinkler system. He was busy, he wasn't paying attention to me, and I just walked away.

There were lovely flowers blooming in the front gardens at *Serenity* and the lawn was freshly cut. But sheets of plywood, painted gray, covered all the windows and doors. Even the eight glass windows of the widow's walk were boarded up. That sad contrast between the bright flowers and the dull gray boards on the windows meant even more to me as I grew older and observed the same contrast between my mother's persistent attempt to please my father and his growing indifference. She brought the light into our world and he turned his back to it the way he turned his back to the *Serenity* cottage. It was my mother, a woman possessing neither a driver's license nor a set of car keys in her life, who hijacked my father's truck and drove me back to the cottage five years later when another wave of sadness swept across America. It was the spring of 1968 and I turned thirteen while the country was mourning the deaths of Martin Luther King and Bobby Kennedy. My father had flown to Canada for his brother's retirement party and my mother and I were alone in the house. On the morning of my birthday she made pancakes and brought a cigar box to the breakfast table in which she had saved mementos from my childhood. My first tooth and a lock of hair. The name-tag I was given on the first day of kindergarten. Beneath a red maple leaf that she and I had waxed when I was six years old was the fingerprinting kit that Sheriff Kane had given me.

She was barefoot, and I still remember her small white hands on the steering wheel and how straight she sat as we drove to Rose Point. First gear gave her some trouble, but other than that she did fine. Her eyes filled with joy when the electric gate slid open for us.

It was her idea that I leave the fingerprints of Mr. Halworth in the mailbox on the front porch of the abandoned cottage. Even as I write this so many years later, I can still recall how certain I was that one day they would return and find them.

4

I moved to California. Los Angeles, which is, in every respect, as far from Maine as you can get. And that was my intention; to put as much distance between myself and my old man as I could. I think about this when I make my way out to Santa Monica beach at sunrise each morning. I think about how we get lost in this life, and then how we find ourselves again. This is the way it happens: We find and refind ourselves again and again in a life, or in an hour. We make plans, take vows, lay out our work clothes on the chair before we get into bed, we charge ahead and fall behind, believing what we need to believe in order to keep marching. And then, without thinking, we turn slightly and suddenly there it is, the story of our life, what we will be remembered for, and what we will remember most vividly at the end. I believe this. I'm forty years old now, you might say old enough to know better. But I still hold on stubbornly to the belief that our lives are more about fate than accommodation.

Having said that, here's my confession: On the lookout

for Fate to take hold of me, I spent a lot of time waiting for my life to begin. Time I won't ever get back.

These things pass through my mind in the early morning hours when I ski from the city out to Santa Monica. I could have become a jogger, and for a while I made my morning pilgrimage on Rollerblades. But when they came out with these three-foot-long skis on wheels, I took up the practice to remind myself that I was from Maine, a skier's paradise, though my father declared it an enthusiasm of the rich and forbade me from ever trying.

I ski without headphones and music so that I can hear the ocean drawing near. The first concussion of waves. The first gull crying overhead. I like the way these sounds reach me by degrees, creating a sense that I have taken a journey from the city to the sea, from darkness into the light.

I try to leave my work behind, but that morning as I passed through the dawn haze along the shore, I was having a difficult time hearing the sea above the dull, persistent roll call of names that was drumming inside my head: *Tom Cruise. Tom Hanks. Tom Petty and the Heartbreakers. Tom Dick, and Harry.*

Just names to me. The names I drop at parties and in restaurants. Names that The Company represents and that I bend over backward for and spend my days promoting and, in the end, hope I don't have to sell my soul for, though better men than I have and will again.

I found my way to The Company ten years ago. It was a long road. I was a banker in St. Paul. A fund-raiser in Des Moines. A systems analyst in Chicago, though I never really knew what *that* was. I sold time-share vacations on the western shore of Lake Michigan for two years, persuading people to swear their faith in an unknown future: *Others may die, others may fall to illness or see their families torn apart by betrayal, but none of that bad stuff can touch me because I'm booked for the same two-weeks' vacation every year for the rest of my life!* The things men do to placate their fears.

By the time I was twenty-nine years old I had enough money saved to return to school and was accepted as a graduate student in the divinity school at the University of Chicago. That was the year two NASA rockets lifted off from Cape Kennedy heading straight up into the sky, traveling five thousand miles an hour *for twelve years* (straight up!) looking for signs of intelligence in the deepest reaches of our solar system. I was searching for something myself; many of us were then. Maybe I just wanted to find proof that life was more than simply a matter of popping out of someone's belly, going back and forth to an office for a while, and ending up in the ground.

Anyway, divinity school didn't work for me, and I went back to work. Five years as a book scout in Manhattan putting together million-dollar deals for studios on the West Coast. Then this headhunter showed up at my office and offered me five times as much money doing pretty much the same thing in Hollywood.

It's the kind of work that can take over your life, and that morning as I rolled past the scenic overlook at Ramsdale Point I was surprised to see a Christmas tree in the window of a coffee shop. It could have been Easter or Halloween as far as I knew. I had long ago become disconnected from the seasons. Or, to be more precise, once I joined the legions of men and women for whom time is money, every day of the week, every month of the year became the same to me. "Time is money" we all said to one another, though I suspect we hoped it was a lot more than that.

I didn't give it another thought that morning at the office. Christmas, I mean. But late in the afternoon, Peter Billings asked me if I wanted to join him and a few of the other guys on a Christmas ski trip to the French Alps. We were pumping away on the Nautilus in a mirrored room at The Club on Bishop Street and trying to hear each other above some piped-in top forties hit by Cher.

"Who else is going?" I asked him.

"Meaning, for chicks?" he said. "Five hot ones from the Merrill Lynch typing pool."

"They still have typing pools?"

Billings finished ten reps at the bench press, then stood for a while in front of the mirrors pushing his thinning hair over his bald spot. "If I died tomorrow," he said suddenly, "who would give a damn that I've spent most of my youth filling the pockets of meat-eating producers with trophy girlfriends? I mean, what's it all worth, anyway?"

Just turned thirty, I said to myself. A few hairs on his pillow in the mornings and the big questions begin to roll in like dark clouds. I was lying on my stomach working the stiffness out of my knees. My cheek was pressed hard against the padded vinyl bench that always smelled exactly like the place mats on the dining room table in my parents' house when I used to lay my head down as a boy and stare at the green vegetables my old man made me eat.

Stories fall out of me, that's one of the reasons I've done so well in the movie business, and the story I gave Peter Billings to try to persuade him how lucky we were to be white men living in America and working our asses off in a lucrative profession in the final years of the twentieth century was about the island off the coast of Maine where some of the country's finest granite had been dug in the 1920s and '30s. "All the men there died of emphysema from the dust," I explained to Billings. "The deal was that once you started coughing up blood you'd go see the foreman and spit on the ground for him. If there was blood in your spit you'd get thirty days off with pay to cut the granite marker for your grave."

"Damn," Billings said with a short laugh. "Is that a true story?"

"None of the men on that island lived to see his fiftieth

birthday," I said. "I'd be in my second to last pair of shoes right now, and you wouldn't still look like a movie star."

I watched him worry another minute about his hair, and then he turned to me and asked what I would do for Christmas if I didn't go skiing in the Alps.

"Work," I said.

"Yeah, I know that story," he said.

5

That night I was at Morton's having dinner with the newest turk to join The Company, another brighter than hell MBA from the Kellogg School in a thousand-dollar suit. His name was Holiday and I was doing my part ushering him into the kingdom and giving him the lay of the land.

"It's about *activity,*" I told him. "You get a script or a novel and you want to stir up as much activity around it as you can. Pull as many potential customers into the orbit as you can. And control the flow of information. Never tell the whole story. Hit the high points, the major reversals. Hook them. You get enough people running around this town with *your* hooks in *their* wallets and you'll make a living."

His expression was so earnest that I was afraid he might actually say "Wow." So I changed the subject before we were both embarrassed.

"What are you doing for Christmas?" I asked him. To my surprise a look of sorrow swept across his face. It was a momentary thing, gone in the next breath, replaced by the cavalier tone that is the common currency of my profession.

"I'll be right here in tinsel town," he recovered and said with a narrow grin.

But your heart will be somewhere else, I thought to myself. And I knew then that he wasn't going to make it at The Company. There was some goodness in him that would dull his ambition and doom him before long.

Outside we stood under the red awning waiting for the valet to bring my car. "I think I'll walk from here," he said, holding out his hand for me to shake.

I watched him walk away down Wilshire Boulevard. I saw him stop and look up at the stars.

The telephone in my car was ringing when the valet pulled to a stop in front of me. A pushy producer with a sweet housekeeping deal on the Paramount lot. In the past two years he'd spent fifty-five million of the studio's money on options that never panned out. He needed a sure thing or he was history.

"There's only one director for this," he told me.

"That's right," I said. "Casey."

"Exactly," he agreed. "Can you get him?"

"The Company represents him, Harry."

"And Nicholson would have to carry the lead."

"He's our client too."

"Okay then. Okay. Let me have some time."

I looked at my watch. It was nine forty-five. "I'll give you until midnight," I said.

He didn't thank me before he hung up.

While I drove down Beverly Boulevard, Bing Crosby was singing "White Christmas" on the radio. At the Myrna Loy building on the Sony lot in Culver City, I dropped off a pair of silver high heels left at my place by a woman I'd stopped dating, then headed home.

Eddie, my doorman, has a weakness for the one thing that could get him fired by the Town House Association—eating on the job—and I pretended not to see him slide a pizza crust into the pocket of the navy blue sport coat he was required to wear.

"Evening Mr. McQuinn," he said, as he recovered and swung the glass door open for me.

"What are you doing for Christmas, Eddie?" I asked.

"I got the day off this year, Mr. McQuinn," he said with alacrity. "Taking my wife and kids to Disneyland."

"This *is* Disneyland," I told him as I stepped into the elevator.

"I hear you, Mr. McQuinn," he said.

A deal can go down at any time. It's like waiting to go into labor, a female colleague with no children of her own once told me. A few years back I closed a $40 million feature with Overland Films in the middle of an earthquake. Tonight I took a shower, got out of one suit and into another, and returned a call to Max Anaman at Boulevard Pictures.

I had already burned up more than an hour in the morning pitching a script to Max. He was one of those guys who had seventeen ways to say no without saying no, and this movie was a tough-sell story about an accountant who gets struck by lightning on a golf course and from that moment on starts sinking putts the pros can't make. He writes a book about putting, quits his job, and travels the country giving demonstrations to thousands of grateful golfers, one of whom turns out to be a former *Playboy* bunny who is very very grateful. Max liked the story line but wanted to change it from golf to basketball.

It was 11:15 when I reached him. He answered his phone just as I was stuffing five or six days' worth of take-out food containers into my kitchen wastebasket.

"Me again, Max."

"Jesus, don't you ever just enjoy yourself?"

"I enjoy myself every time I talk to you," I said.

"I bet," he said.

"I want you to start thinking differently about golf, Max. It can be an action sport."

Max laughed.

"Max," I said. "You've got to start thinking about golf in a different way."

I was listening to his reply and checking HBO and Cinemax to see if there was anything decent on tonight when the call-waiting began beeping.

"I need to take another call, Max," I said. "Can I get back to you in ten minutes?"

"Take your call; I'm going bowling," he said.

Before I tell you what happened next, I should explain why I hadn't heard my father's voice in ten years. But such a thing can't really be explained. Ten years ago my mother passed away. I flew home for the funeral, and rather than sleep one night in the same house or the same town or the same state as my father, I drove back to the airport and spent the rest of the night sitting at the gate waiting for morning to come.

My father and I split up because of money, I think. Money and pride. As I grew up I began to see that my old man really had no life of his own, and he deprived my mother of a life as well. She wanted to travel a little, see a new place, but he closed the door on every possibility and he resented her for asking. He called himself a caretaker at Rose Point, but for giving every day of his life to the rich summer people, I called him a servant. Once to his face. And when he took a swing at me for it, I stepped back and then caught him on the chin with a punch that knocked him over the foot of my bed. How do you ever get beyond something like that? You can't.

It came to a head the year I turned seventeen. That winter he had worked twelve-hour days for months building a new addition on the cottage called *Fourwinds*, which was owned by a judge from Florida who I'd seen a few times and despised for his red pants and the little gold insignia on the breast pocket of his green blazer. Three days before he was due to arrive for Memorial Day weekend, I took the key to the place from my old man's workshop and filled the judge's new bed with soft-shell clams. When he arrived, the smell in that part of the house was so bad my father had to tear the addition down. And here's the thing: When he found out that I'd done it, he reported me to the police.

After that, there was no turning back for either of us. The months turned into years, and then I said good-bye to my mother.

Tonight it was my father on call-waiting. "I've got my doctor here," he said. "He wants to talk to you."

That was it. I could have hung up.

"Your father's in the hospital," the doctor told me. "I don't think he's going to make it."

Two hours later I was on the red-eye flight, drinking a vodka tonic and remembering my trip home to Maine when my mother was in the final stages of cancer. I had spent the last hours of her life in a chair by her bed. Exhausted from the trip, I had nodded off, and to my surprise she woke me up and asked me to come closer. She patted my head and said, "My boy, my boy." I looked into her bloodshot eyes and knew in that instant that I was one of those sons who had made a far better boy than a man.

What I'm saying is, I realized then that I had never grown up.

As the plane rose into the night sky I started making phone calls to cover for my absence the next day. I was on the phone until we crossed the Rocky Mountains, my face against the portal window so I could watch the moon floating by. The in-flight movie was one I'd packaged seven years ago, and knowing the people who were stabbed in the back to get the film made took the fun out of it for me. I turned on the music instead.

"Each time you pass down the aisle," I whispered to the first-class attendant, "please bring me another vodka tonic. I'm going to need at least seven of these to conk out."

She wore a little too much purple eye shadow. Another woman who, like so many of the women in my industry, had passed through that short period of time when beauty came naturally, and now was trying too hard. What could be more cruel than *time*? Time which, for a while, is benevolent, each month, each year making you more beautiful, before it turns against you, like a guest you've invited into your home who ends up stealing your silverware and jewelry on his way out. Time, the Trojan horse.

As she turned away I told her I was sorry. "I don't mean to be a problem for you. It's just that this is a rough trip for me."

She managed a smile. I looked around the compartment at the other first-class passengers and I wondered, as I often do, how many of these people had become prosperous on their own, the way I had. It's one of the hazards of a competitive life like mine, this kind of measuring, and it always leaves me feeling anxious. But I can't help it; it means a lot to me that I worked my way to the top without the benefit of a trust fund or a helping hand. I earned my way through college playing football. I've got a pinky finger that I cannot bend and screws in one ankle to show for it. I fought my way to the top. Why does this matter? And what does it say about me that I still draw some kind of cold consolation from it?

I don't know. Some men take satisfaction, I suppose, in announcing to the world that they are more successful than their fathers were before them. What I wanted was to reach a point where I could afford to *hire* my father *to work for me* if I wanted. And those rich summer people from my boyhood, I'm still trying to measure up to them. Which is why I paid a lot of money to fill my driveway in Beverly Hills with crushed seashells the way the cottage driveways are at Rose Point.

I closed my eyes. "Hate yourself," I said below my breath. "But don't take it out on other people."

I had just fallen asleep when a baby began crying somewhere behind me. I got out of my seat and walked back through the dark blue drapes separating first class from the rest of the passengers. There I found people packed together, struggling to sleep or to wake up. They had the look of survivors of some terrible hardship. When I saw the woman with the crying baby in her arms I began walking toward her without really thinking what I was going to say or do.

She smiled up at me. *Smiled*, despite her discomfort.

"Why don't you take my seat up front?" I said to her.

She didn't want to impose, she said, but I insisted. I helped her carry her bags and get settled. When I closed the overhead compartment and looked down, the baby was staring into my eyes.

I will tell you this, though it is not easy for me to admit. That was the first decent thing I had done for anyone in a long time.

6

At the airport in Boston I bought a newspaper, had my shoes shined, and waited for a small commuter plane to take me the rest of the way. When the plane was ready for boarding I dropped my ticket in a trash can. It just came over me that I didn't want to get there that quickly. I needed time to think.

It was cold in Boston, that relentless New England cold that makes your bones feel brittle. I rented a car and drove out of the city, north on Route 1, passing the Boston waterfront where tankers and container ships filled with oil from the Middle East and junk from Asia were tied to wharfs. Morning traffic was heavy. Both outbound lanes of the highway were crowded with businessmen in a hurry to get somewhere.

I had just crossed the New Hampshire border into Maine when I began thinking of the psychiatrist I saw for a while after my mother's death. I remembered her in skintight leather pants telling me that I was going to need long-term counseling in order to come to terms with the destruction in my past. I didn't get this at all; with everything that I possessed and all the chances I had been given, how could anyone say I'd had a rough life? I know that depression is real and that some people suffer terribly from diseases of the mind, but in my case it wasn't depression, it was cowardice. When I told the doctor this, she tilted her head and said, "Maybe you're right."

I could see her face when I gazed into the deep, empty blue sky ahead of me. But I couldn't picture my old man. His face had vanished from my consciousness long before.

I was staring into the sky when the tollbooth operator yelled at me. "Mister?"

I looked at her. "You have to pay me," she said.

I took Mud River Road through Biddeford (the long way), and when the medical center appeared up ahead I couldn't push my foot down on the gas pedal. I turned off the road onto the gravel shoulder and sat there. I wondered if anyone ever succeeds in outrunning his past. One of the few remaining miracles about America is that you can leave one life and start a new one in the blink of an eye if you have a few credit cards. We don't even have to say good-bye to our neighbors because we never knew them. And we won't be homesick for the place we're leaving behind because in the new place there will be an identical strip mall with Big Macs and office supplies from Staples to make us feel safe.

On the way to the hospital I stopped at a grocery store and bought a can of cashews. That was the only thing I could ever give my old man. Cashews on his birthday. Cashews on Father's Day, and Christmas. He was a neat man, meaning he hated clutter, and I think a gift of cashews was perfect because he could eat them and throw the can away, and that would be that. No trace of his son's gift, no awful neckties or ceramic ashtrays to hold on to until his child went off to college.

A heavyset woman at the visitors' desk inside the glass lobby went down a list of patients' names. She lost her smile and told me it would take another minute. She made a call, and just as she finished telling me that it looked like we would have a white Christmas a woman in a plaid jumper appeared and told me she was very sorry but my father had died in the night. I knew I had heard her correctly, but I asked anyway. "He died? Are you sure?"

She told me that she was sorry, and said yes, she was sure.

I made my way to the hospital morgue, passing nurses and janitors and patients in flimsy paper slippers.

Seeing my father in the drawer that pulled out of the refrigerator, his body so much smaller than I remembered it, and holding his folded khaki shirt and pants in my hands, the uniform he always wore, I felt small. And alone. When your parents are alive you feel that you still have a ways to go on this earth. When they're gone, you know that the umbrella of immunity has been lifted from your head.

The technician, whose white lab coat was stained with grease and mustard, asked me if I wanted burial or cremation. It was up to me to decide this for my father, a man who had always decided everything for himself and his wife and for me when I lived under his roof. I'm getting even now, Pop, I thought.

I chose the less time-consuming of the two. "You can pick up the remains tomorrow by four," he said.

"Not till then?" I asked.

He looked surprised. "Can you mail them to me?" I said. He took my address, and I left the can of cashews on a chair.

Later, in my father's house I played his old Sinatra records, drank some of his apricot brandy, and thought about when one of the older guys in my office had died not long ago. We all followed the office custom of putting yellow Post-it notes on his door the next day. I wrote a passage from Shelly's "Ode on a Grecian Urn" on mine, which reminded me that I still didn't know the details surrounding that poet's death in Italy in the nineteenth century and I probably wouldn't ever have the time to find out.

I was on the telephone with my secretary, standing at the living room window that looked out across an empty snow-covered field, when I remembered that the only other time I'd been in the city hospital before today was when a rich man dressed like Santa Claus had taken me there.

7

Later that day a man from the auction house on Payne Road met me at my father's house.

"I could write you a check for three thousand, for everything, right here," the man said. "More than three grand and I have to go back to the boss for authorization."

His name was Sergeant. He was maybe thirty-five and had long sideburns that had been fashionable in another era. He wore a cashmere coat and big boots that tracked snow through my father's house.

"I was thinking more along the lines of eight thousand for everything," I told him.

He grimaced. "I'm including the cost of getting rid of some of it. They closed down the dump here, maybe you didn't know that."

That edgy tone—right out of some correspondence course in negotiations offered by a no-name business school.

"So what will you have to dispose of?"

"All the appliances, for starters."

"You can't resell them?"

"People won't buy used anymore. They see the new ones on TV and they want them. Plus all the clothing, there's no market for that."

I was looking past him to a photograph of my mother that stood in a frame on an end table. In the picture she was about my own age now, and even from where I stood I could see myself in her face.

"I'm pretty sure we'll have to dispose of most of the rugs," I heard him say.

"So, you're saying it's trash then, right? The remains of two people's lives?"

I watched his face turn red.

He was going to pay three thousand; I wanted eight. The difference of five thousand is about what I tack on my expense account every month. "All right," I said. "But I want everything out of here by the end of the day tomorrow."

He grimaced again. "Tomorrow? I don't know."

"Has to be tomorrow."

He looked around as if he was thinking it over. I knew he wasn't going to walk away.

"How soon can I start removing stuff?" he asked.

"Right now."

After he left I picked up the photograph of my mother and looked at it more carefully. The same nose. The same creases at the corners of her eyes. My color hair. It's funny how you think of your life as pretty much a straight line until you see it begin to bend into a circle.

It wasn't a big job; my father was not a man to save much. I spent two hours with a realtor, another two with a lawyer who would settle my father's estate—his cash assets were just under twenty thousand dollars, my base monthly income—had a quick lunch, and by the time I returned to the house everything but the rugs and one floor lamp was gone.

I could have left then. I mean, I could have driven back to Boston and flown home. Instead I walked through the empty rooms of my father's house, listening to the echo of my footsteps in the stillness. I thought of my mother starting her life in this house. In her early twenties, just married to Pop. What had she wanted then? What had she dreamed of having and doing in this world?

There were ghosts in the empty rooms. Over there, by the door that opened to the attic stairs is where my mother kept her sewing machine. I remembered the spring my father promised her a vacation to the Finger Lakes after the summer people had gone home. All summer she sewed new outfits for the trip. Sometime in late August the sewing machine broke and my father refused to give her the money to repair it. By then he had decided to pull the plug on the vacation, anyway. I was working as a life-guard on Higgins Beach that summer, and I snuck the sewing machine out of the house and paid to have it fixed. My mother was pleased, but I never saw her sitting at the machine again.

On the back of a closet door were the pencil markings she made to measure my height from year to year. Standing before this door, I recalled her pleasure in this ritual. How she smiled and how eager I was to turn around and see how I had grown.

I touched the mark for September 1967. Five feet, four inches. I closed my eyes and there is my mother standing in front of me in her red plaid housedress. The radio is on, and just as she makes the mark on the door there is a news bulletin that three astronauts have burned to death in the capsule on the launchpad in Florida. My mother drops the pencil.

In the kitchen I saw my father. The way he was always wiping the counters with a dishcloth even when they were spotless. His annoying habit of checking to see that I hadn't left a burner on or the refrigerator door open. If he could slide a dollar bill into the freezer after I'd closed the door, then I hadn't closed it tight enough and was costing him money.

It was two o'clock when I left the key in the realtor's lockbox and walked away from the house. At the town Mobile station I asked if I could leave my father's truck with a for sale sign in the windshield. "I'll give you a twenty percent commission on whatever it sells for," I told the red-haired boy behind the counter, who took this offer eagerly and then gave me a ride back to my car. I noticed the dirt under his fingernails. The calluses on his palms. Working hands like my old man's. Not like my own.

By four o'clock I was on the interstate heading south when I remembered that I had left the photograph of my mother on the table in the living room; it had been carted away with all the rest of the furniture. From the moment I had stepped onto the plane to fly east all I had in mind was a clean break. But now I began driving slower, thinking about going back. It was crazy, I know, but I turned around at the next exit.

The auction house was closed when I got there. I called the number that was stenciled on the glass door and pleaded my case to a man with a soft voice; he told me to wait there, he would meet me in ten minutes.

"It's silly, I know," I said, when he arrived.

"It isn't silly at all," he said, taking a key from his cash drawer. "People change their minds all the time. About ten years ago we started a practice of keeping everything in the back barn for forty-eight hours before we dispose of it."

He was gracious enough to leave me alone, and though I paused over my mother's rolling pin and a wig she'd worn after her cancer treatment, I ended up taking only the photograph.

8

From the moment I held my mother's picture in my hand I knew what I wanted to do with it. Instead of heading to the interstate, I drove out the Blackpoint Road to Rose Point.

I left my car outside the locked gate and walked six or seven hundred yards on Winslow Homer Lane to my father's shop.

It was a small act of defiance on my part, and I did it for my mother. During the forty-nine years my old man worked at Rose Point this shop was his kingdom, a place my mother was never welcome. I found the key in an old soup can under the third step. When I leaned against the door, all I planned to do before I got back in my car was hammer a nail into one of the studs and hang the picture on it so that whoever was hired to take over my old man's caretaking position would look up from time to time at my mother in her rose-patterned dress, and wonder. Just wonder, that's all.

The door swung open on its bronze hinges, and I could not move. I smelled oil and wood shavings. On the floor in front of me, my father's footprints in sawdust. I turned away and stared out at the ocean to try and clear my head. Suddenly I wanted to be back in California drinking vodka tonics in the bar at the Beverly Hills Hilton. Sitting by the piano watching the supermodels chain-smoke to keep themselves thin. I tried to picture myself there, thinking that I would never have to return to Maine again. Maybe I would buy a bigger house near the beach now, or maybe I'd move into the Wilshire Hotel into one of their long-term luxury suites. I'd grow old there, and mark the shifting economics of the world by the changing nationality of the bellhops who brought me room service.

But the moment I stepped inside I felt all of that fall out of me. I stood in my father's world, in a silence and stillness that seemed to have descended just as I opened the shop door. It was as if a wind had rushed through the room ahead of me, and now everything had just settled back in its place.

I walked to the band saw, with its dull green casing. Another two steps to the table saw where a pair of goggles hung from the iron fence. Then the miter box where my father had taught me to cut angles. The grinding wheel where we sharpened our chisels in a shower of white sparks. The overhead racks of mahogany and cedar. The old oak roll-top desk, its drawers filled with hardware. With my eyes closed I could still name everything in those drawers.

It was a tidy shop, all the tools within reach like the galley of a ship. I walked solemnly, breathing in the rich scent of pine. As a boy I had stood in this room with my father. Hadn't I dreamed of one day becoming him before we became so angry at one another? He was an uncomplicated man who had grown up on a potato farm in Canada, a day's drive from here but a million miles away. In the privileged world of Rose Point he must have felt out of place, and yet, lucky. Fortunate to have found a way to earn his passage as a man in such a quiet and beautiful place. His own boss, so to speak. This desk, this shop, these tools that were once new to him and then became the center of his life had satisfied whatever desires carried him from his father's world. This was his Hollywood. I saw that now for the first time. He had left his own father's world to come here, and I had left his world to go somewhere else. Seeing this, letting it sink into my consciousness, opened some part of me. It was a small opening, but I felt it.

There was the telephone at the workbench with the numbers worn off the dial. And across the double windows that gave my father an ocean view, a length of twine with clothespins hanging from it where he clipped his work orders, each on a slip of paper, like a short-order cook.

One slip of paper still hung there. When I saw it I thought it must be the job he would have finished next if he hadn't died. How unlike my father it was to leave a job unfinished.

Before I crossed the room to read the work order, I

wondered if it was something my father didn't like doing, some job he was putting off for another day. Or if he had just forgotten to take the paper down. I won't say that I had a premonition about what was written on that slip of paper. But there was something: Just as I took it in my hand, I glanced out the window above the desk and saw that it had begun to snow.

The words were written in my father's left-handed script. Words that stopped my heart:

Open *Serenity* for Christmas

Below these words, a telephone number.

In a movie the actor would show his surprise by raised eyebrows, perhaps a gasp or a hand reaching for his heart. I just stood there reading the words over and over, maybe thinking that if I read them enough times it would all come clear to me. I backed away, a step or two, then turned and ran.

I ran the way a boy would run, straight out the door without stopping to close it behind me. I ran without looking at the ground to see if there was anything in my way. At the end of the lane I could see the bare flagpole in front, and when the first part of the porch came into my view I was already expecting to see that my father had opened the cottage. But it stood exactly as I remembered it, boarded up, abandoned.

For a long time I stood in the falling snow, thinking about how far I had ventured from this place and the person I had been when I had last seen the *Serenity* cottage. The years now seemed to have passed quickly. Summers lost and gone. I wondered if my father had felt the same loss at the end, if he had been surprised at how quickly his time had passed.

Snow collected on my shoulders as I stood looking at the cottage. My plane was going to leave Boston in three hours. Back home I had suits to pick up at the dry cleaners in the morning and at least a dozen people I needed to call. And tennis at the club tomorrow night. A busy life that suddenly felt like it didn't belong to me.

9

I took the work order from the line of string and a carpenter's pencil from the desk drawer and then I dialed the number my father had written down. While it rang I looked out at the low clouds gathering above the harbor. The area code was for New York City. After four rings there was a taped message, two sentences in a child's voice: "Nobody is here. Leave beeps for Mommy."

Leave beeps. I laughed out loud. There are no children in the world that I inhabit, and this child's voice had caught me by such surprise that I hadn't listened carefully and didn't know if it was a boy or girl.

"All right," I said. "Here are my beeps—BEEP, BEEP. Please have your mommy call the caretaker at Rose Point." I paused, and then added stupidly, "In Maine."

I waited a few seconds on the empty line, as if I thought the child might speak again. For some reason I didn't want to hang up.

Then I clipped the work order back on the string where

my father had left it. I turned it so I could read the words while I sat in my father's chair and waited.

I waited fifteen minutes. I told myself I would wait fifteen more. I read the words again:

Open *Serenity* for Christmas.

The shop was cold and growing colder. There were a few dry logs in one corner of the room. I split them into kindling with my father's ax and started a fire in the woodstove. The room was nearly filled with smoke before I found the damper on the stovepipe. I had to open the door to clear the air. The temperature outside had fallen. Either that, or the cold was getting to me after so many years of comfort in LA. The sky had filled in with dark clouds, but off in the west, just above the horizon, there was a ribbon of bright pink light. "Red sky at night," I said to myself. But I couldn't recall the rest of it. I remembered the disdain that my father had for all TV and radio meteorologists. "Stand outside before you go to bed," he would say, "and you'll be able to forecast tomorrow's weather yourself." Since college I had my football knees to predict humidity and rain, and today they felt like they were made of wood.

I checked my watch again. Twenty minutes more. Another hour and I would miss my flight.

Because in my life I never sit still, I was fighting back the persistent urge to get up and do something. The trick to living alone is to keep moving from the minute you open your eyes in the morning, charging ahead at full speed so that at the end of the day you're too exhausted to think about anything, especially what you might have missed. If there's another way to keep from being lonely, I haven't found it.

Finally, I walked across the room and stood in the doorway of the shop listening to the stillness around me, a kind of universal quiet that made me feel awkward and nervous. I thought a moment and then yelled at the top of my lungs, "Merry Christmas to all!" I had somehow forgotten how alone you could be in Maine, and how it felt to be so alone. I yelled once more, half expecting my words to change something this time. But they disappeared into the sky, and the stillness returned.

Back to the desk. Back to the chair.

Open *Serenity* for Christmas.

Ten more glances at my watch. Five more minutes and I gave it up. Forget it, I thought, and I went outside with a bucket that I filled with snow to douse the fire in the woodstove.

I was on my knees putting snow on the hot coals when the telephone rang. In the world I know, eagerness is seen as weakness and so my habit is to always let the telephone ring twice. And then a third time.

I answered and heard a woman's voice speaking my father's name.

"Paul McQuinn, please?" she said.

My father had always been known by the summer residents of Rose Point as Mister Mac.

"I'm his son," I said.

"His son?" she said. "When I spoke with your father he didn't tell me he had a son working with him."

"I don't work here," I told her.

"Excuse me?"

Excuse me, I thought. And I felt myself losing my patience. "You're not from around here," I said. "These people don't call my father by his name."

"I don't understand," she said.

"Look," I said, "I'm here from California because my father died."

"Mr. McQuinn?"

"Yes, my father. I'm leaving later today. Tonight, I mean. I have a flight out tonight and I'm just here tying up loose ends."

"I just spoke with your father on Monday," she said. *"Now he's gone?"*

She said this with such compassion that it caught me off guard and I couldn't think of what to say to this. "I liked your message," I told her.

"Message?"

"On the answering machine."

For a moment she said nothing. Then, "Oh. Yes. That's my Olivia."

"Olivia," I said in a distracted way, glancing out the window at the falling snow.

"It's a rather big name for a little girl," she said. "But she'll grow into it."

I told her flatly that I was sure she would, then I asked her if she was coming to Maine.

"I'm just so sorry to hear about your father," she said, as if she hadn't heard me.

"His heart was bad," I said, a little too glibly.

There was only silence. And then she replied. "I'm . . . I'm so sorry," she said quietly.

I heard the loneliness in her voice. Or was it sadness, I wondered. A genuine sadness for my father's death. That she seemed vulnerable in some way kept me from coming right out and asking her who she was. "Did you know my father?" I asked.

"I never knew him," she told me. "But as I said, we spoke on the telephone on Monday."

"Yes. So you own *Serenity* cottage?"

"Well," she said, and then she hesitated. "It's a long story."

"*Long?*" I said. "Or *old.*"

"Yes," she said as if she trusted me. "Both. You're right."

Suddenly everything was so quiet I could hear her breathing.

"Is it beautiful there?" she asked me.

"It is," I said. "Some people think there's no more

beautiful place in the world. Didn't your . . ." I paused, and then decided to ask. "Didn't your father ever tell you about Rose Point?"

"My father?" she said.

And it was how she turned those two words into a question, not stating the words, but asking them—*my father?*—that made me know at once that this was Charles Halworth's daughter, the little girl preserved so clearly in my memory that I could still picture her in her shiny shoes. I stood up at my father's desk and closed my eyes. Then I sat down again. Here I was, not a boy setting mouse-traps with my father but a man shot across the sky at thirty-three thousand feet from California to Maine to hear, against all odds, a woman's voice that belonged to the daughter Charles Halworth called Katie when he promised thirty years ago that the two of them were going to teach me to skate on Christmas day. I had spent perhaps five hours with her, sitting beside her in her father's big car, walking next to her in the toy store, following her down the hospital corridors. Five hours, thirty years ago. The past. The past suddenly returning to me with such force of emotion that I can no longer think of the past as merely a time, but also a place.

"Yes," I said.

"I'm afraid I only found out about Rose Point a few weeks ago. I explained it to your father. He and I had a good laugh together," she said. "The cottage belonged to my mother. When she remarried last month and moved to

England with her new husband, she went through her things. As she put it, it was time for housecleaning. You'd have to know her to appreciate that."

I smiled at this and felt a kind of anticipation rising inside me, the same boyish excitement that had sent me running to the cottage when I first saw the work order. "And she gave the cottage to you?"

"She said it was an old, musty place too close to the sea to ever get the bath towels to dry properly." She laughed. "That's my mother through and through, Mr. McQuinn."

"And your father?" I asked her again.

"That was part of my mother's housecleaning as well," she said. "My father left her before I was born, but it seems that he and my mother once spent time at Rose Point. I just found that out. I suppose that's why she forgot about the place. Bad memories and all. In any event, Mr. McQuinn, I need to come and see this place now that I know the truth about it."

The truth, I thought, was a lie.

"What did my father say when you told him?" I asked her.

"Just that he understood."

"And did he say he would open the cottage for you?" I asked.

"Yes," she said.

"For Christmas?"

"Yes. For Christmas."

Her voice faded with the mention of Christmas. And I thought I detected a contradiction in her, as if she were hoping and giving up at the same time.

"Then I'll have the place ready for you," I said.

"I don't know," she said.

"What?"

"How can I ask you to do this? With your father dying? And you need to go home?"

"You didn't ask me. I offered."

"But are you sure?"

I was no longer listening. "When do you want to arrive?"

"Well," she said, "I had planned to drive up on the twentieth. And stay until the day after Christmas. That's what I told Mr. McQuinn. I'm sorry . . . your father."

"The twentieth? So, five days from today?"

"Yes, but are you sure?"

"Fine," I said.

"What's your name?"

"Excuse me?"

"Your name?"

"Terry," I said.

"I'm Katherine," she said. "You're very kind, but if our visit is too much of an imposition . . ."

"No, it won't be. It's not going to be an imposition."

"So, I'll get to meet you then?"

"I'll be waiting with your keys."

"Oh," she said, "I have keys; I nearly forgot. My mother gave me keys."

"There's an electric gate," I explained.

"That sounds dreadful," she said. "Is it necessary?"

"It discourages the wild bears," I said.

"Bears?"

"No," I said. "It's not necessary, but it's there."

"Let me check the keys," she said. "I'll be right back. Okay?"

I heard a train whistle in the distance. I opened the doors on the woodstove and pushed the logs back farther with my foot. The room I was standing in seemed transformed in some way, the way a room can after a stranger walks through it.

When she came back on the line she told me the key ring had two keys, one much smaller than the other.

"Yes, the small one would be for the gate," I told her. "I'll have to guess on which rooms to make up."

"Anything will be fine," she said.

"The cottage has twelve bedrooms," I said.

"Twelve! That's a little daunting."

"Daunting, yes. How many rooms should I make up?"

"Two," she said.

"Two," I said, knowing that the math was simple. One room for the child. One for the mother and father. The wife and husband.

"One for Olivia and me, and the other for our friend who helps us."

A friend, no husband? I thought.

"And a room for you, if you'll be staying with us," she said, pleasantly.

"I'll be staying in town," I said. "I'll make up two rooms with ocean views, how's that?"

"Are you sure?"

"I'm promising you ocean views. Just like a five-star hotel."

She laughed at this, and I could tell she was happy.

"Well, I'm a very good tipper," she said. "You can tell the bellhops that I'm positively lavish when it comes to tipping."

"Good," I said, "because I'm your bellhop."

She laughed again. "You'll call me if this becomes too much," I heard her say.

"I will," I said. "I'll call you. And you've got my number here?"

"Yes."

I gave her the number of my cellphone as well. She thanked me again, and we said good-bye. I hung up the telephone. Across the room the dark window held my reflection. Beyond it an airplane moved across the sky from star to star. I thought of the airport in Boston and the plane that would take me back home, and my car waiting in the parking lot, and my office. All of that suddenly felt far away, separated from me by more than miles and hours, more than space and time. The voice of Charles Halworth's daughter had crossed life's wide arc of possibilities and reached me as I always believed it would.

I glanced at the work order that I had been writing on while we talked. And I saw that I had written a list of names. The names of actresses who could play Katherine, and actors who would play her father, and the two studio producers I trusted to handle this movie sensitively.

I called Billings, the only friend I trusted at the company.

"Where are you?" he asked.

"Maine."

"Maine? You're not working in that granite quarry?"

"What?"

"The place you told me about where the workers spit up blood, and . . ."

I cut him off and I laid out the story of Katherine Halworth and her father. When it comes to the idea behind a great movie, you know you have something if you can describe it in one declarative sentence.

"Amazing," Billings said. "It would be meat on the table for Crossworth at Sunmount. Say it again?"

"It is a movie about a daughter who finds the father she never knew she had."

"Yeah, wonderful, that is truly wonderful."

"And it would be true, Peter," I said. "All of it."

"So, the father's come back to Maine? Have you met him?"

I told him that part we would have to make up.

"We'd have to get Anthony Terrell to play the father," he said.

"I agree."

"Okay, I'm moving on it. We'll talk again soon."

"Right," I said.

Breaking the speed limit the whole way, I drove into town to see about finding someone to help me open the cottage. From the car I left messages with Sara Burke's manager and her agent. Sara had been the talk of the Toronto Film Festival this past fall for her role as a daughter caring for her dying mother. To get a movie made these days it's imperative to get a star of her caliber attached to it from the outset. I had the work order with me and I kept looking at it. There were my father's words: Open *Serenity* for Christmas. And now there were mine. Names of people who could take someone's life and turn it into a great movie.

10

At the hardware store in town a kid behind a cash register said he had a cousin who needed work. I used the pay phone outside the store. I was so full of adrenaline that I was tapping my foot to the cadence of the phone ringing in my ear. When I got him on the line I told him that the work would take him four days.

"Four days?" he said. "Sounds more like ten to me."

"It has to be done by the twentieth," I told him.

"That means I'd have to start tomorrow."

"That's right."

"I'd have to be paid cash."

Meaning under the table so he could continue to collect his unemployment from the mill.

"What do you charge?"

"For this job? Two grand for the whole of it."

In my world, the value of a person's work is determined only by what someone else is willing to pay for it. The purest form of supply-and-demand economics.

"I'll work with you," I said.

"You a carpenter?"

"No."

"What kind of work do *you* do?"

"Hollywood work," I said. I heard him laugh derisively.

"Must be nice," he said.

I shifted into the gear that carries me through most of my life. "Do you want the work or not?" I said.

He said he would have to think about it.

"You do that," I told him. "I'll call you back in half an hour."

"My wife won't be home 'til tonight. I have to ask her first."

In my work people will waste your time if you let them. "I'm sure your wife would rather have you lying around the living room in your underwear," I said. "I'll find somebody else."

I heard him say, "Hey, what the—" as I hung up on him.

I stood outside the hardware store looking down main street. Not much had changed since I was a boy here. In small towns in Maine many things change, and yet everything always stays the same. And this is true of the men who populate these towns. There is a collection of guys like the guy on the telephone who drop out of high school, buy hammers, and call themselves carpenters. Most of them do shabby work. You see them up and down the coast of Maine, doing odd jobs for the summer people.

Guys who don't take care of their tools and who show the cracks of their rear ends when they bend over. My father used to call them *actors*. That was the word he used to disparage anyone he thought was pretending to be something he wasn't. He died, I was sure, placing me among that feckless cast of pretenders.

I went back inside the store, thinking that I would ask the cashier for another name.

"Any luck?" I heard him say. "Can my cousin give you a hand?"

"No," I said. "He didn't want the work."

An older man at the next register turned toward us. "What kind of work do you have?" he asked me.

"I've got to open up one of the cottages at Rose Point," I told him.

He looked puzzled. "What about McQuinn?" he said. "He's the caretaker out there."

"He died last night," I told him.

"*What?*"

"He's my father, that's what *I'm* doing here."

"Oh man, I'm sorry to hear that," he said. "Your father was a tough old S.O.B., but I liked him."

"Thanks," I said. "Do you know anybody?"

He thought for a minute, then told me there was a guy in Old Orchard Beach who used to come into the store with my father from time to time. "Older guy. He bought the carousel at the fairgrounds a few years ago. I think your father was helping him restore the place. I can try and get in touch with him if you want."

"Great," I said. "Call me." I gave him my cellphone number. "And have you got the number for my father's shop?"

"It's around here somewhere," he said. "I'll call you."

I checked into a motel on Route 1 and paid the manager in advance for five nights. Inside room number 9 I stood looking at the desk beside the bed where I would put my wallet and briefcase. And through the open bathroom door I could see the glass shelf above the sink where I would put my razor and shaving cream. I would stay in this room for five nights, and then I would leave and someone else would take the room for a night or a week. Someone passing through on the way to some other place.

It wasn't good enough. It felt wrong. I had come all this way to a motel room that could have been anywhere. Which meant that it was nowhere. If I was going to make a movie, I needed to be close enough to the Halworth's story for some of my blood to run into it.

11

I did some shopping in a Kmart at the outskirts of town. It had been my mother's favorite store. I was thinking about her red change purse when a woman in a brown smock with a name tag over her heart rang up my purchases. A sleeping bag and a foam-rubber mat to go under it. I had chosen the most expensive in the store, and when I laid down my gold American Express card the woman told me the sleeping bag was good to forty below zero. "In case you ever decide to climb Mount Everest," she said, when she looked up at me.

I wasn't really paying attention, but she hesitated when she read the name on my credit card and when I looked at her she was holding back a smile.

"You don't remember me?" she said.

Our eyes met. There were so many names in my life. "I should remember you," I said to be polite.

"Algebra with Miss Dunne?" she said.

"Algebra with Miss Dunne. Yes, there's a name I remember. Miss Dunne. But, no, I apologize."

She looked down at her name tag. "After a ten-hour

shift I have to remind myself. Gwen Stevens," she said, and she gave me her hand to shake.

I could tell she was a little hurt. "I do remember you," I lied. "How are you?"

"I heard about your father," she said sweetly. "I'm sorry."

I nodded and thanked her, and she told me that she had wondered if I'd come home.

"How did you hear?" I said.

"One of my aunts works at the hospital," she said, nodding with a knowing expression. "I was painting at Rose Point the other summer."

"I didn't know you were a painter," I said stupidly.

"No," she said, "not an artist. Just a housepainter. I used to see your father almost every day. He was always friendly to me. He told me that you were working in Hollywood. He was very pleased, I could tell."

This took me by surprise, and I didn't know what to say. "And how have you been?" I asked. "Using your algebra much?"

She laughed and told me that she had been married and divorced. "No kids," she said. "That made it easier. But you're in Hollywood? That's something. I could tell even back in ninth grade that you were going places."

"It's not as glamorous as it sounds."

"Don't tell me," she said, with a smile. "Don't spoil it for me."

"All right, I won't. But what about you?"

"Me? I'm still here. It's home, I guess."

"There," I said. "Home. That's good."

Our eyes met again. She seemed to understand what I meant.

"So, where are you going now, Terry?" she asked.

When I didn't answer right away she gestured to the sleeping bag.

"Not Mount Everest," I said. For a moment I thought I wouldn't tell her anything. Keep it fast. Make my exit. But then I told her that I was going to be around for a while. "I'm doing some work out at Rose Point that my father couldn't finish," I said.

"Oh, it's so nice there. In one of the cottages?"

"The big place," I said.

"They're *all* big."

"Right, they are. It's the place that's been boarded up."

"Oh, wow," she exclaimed. "Your father told me the story of that house. Amazing, isn't it. And you know, I remember reading about the accident when it happened. Not *me* reading, really, but my dad used to have breakfast with me in the mornings and he'd read me the newspaper."

"What did my father tell you about the cottage?"

"Just that he closed it up after the accident and nobody had been inside it since. So, what do you need the sleeping bag for?"

I told her that I was going to stay at my father's shop.

And she was struck by this. "That's amazing," she said. "That's just wicked nice of you. I mean, to care so much. Your father would really be proud of you."

She was nodding her head the whole time I was telling her that I wasn't so sure he would be.

Then she said, "Sure he would. You know, Terry, there were kids in high school who used to think you were, I don't know, stuck up or something. You did have a chip on your shoulder, I think. But I always knew you had a big heart."

"I'm embarrassed," I said.

"No, don't be. Because it's true. I mean you've been out in Hollywood for all this time, and here you are willing to get your hands dirty to help your father. Not many people would do that, do you think?"

"Well . . . ," I said.

"Hey," she said, "maybe you can turn this into a movie?" Then she quickly laughed. "God, can you imagine?"

A man in a shirt and tie passed by us, eyeing her.

"My manager," she said.

The top of my head was burning and I felt like my legs were going to give out.

We shook hands again and said good-bye. I walked away. I had to stop at the door and take hold of it to keep from either falling down or racing out of the store like some madman.

I practically drove off the road. I stopped for some groceries at a 7-Eleven. "You forgot your change," the cashier called out to me.

"Keep it," I said, as I went out the door.

I don't remember parking outside the gate at Rose Point that night, or walking to my father's shop to drop off the things I'd bought in town. Suddenly it was midnight, and I was standing in the snow looking up at the cottage. Above the highest roof peak a sickle of moon lay on its back. The tall cedar trees were tossing in a light breeze off the ocean. I began thinking about everything my old high school classmate had told me. What would she think if she knew the truth about me? That my first impulse when I heard Katherine Halworth telling me her story was no more honorable than a shark going for blood. That I was always looking out for myself, for a way to distinguish myself from all the people who lead unremarkable lives. Wasn't that the reason I went to Hollywood in the first place? And hadn't I come home *for myself* as well? There wasn't anything I had wanted to say to my father; I was just coming home to hear *him* say something *to me* before he died. Maybe that he was sorry.

Soon my mind was racing through everything that had happened in the last twenty-four hours. I thought about Katherine Halworth as a small child, riding in the backseat of her father's car, sitting next to me with her head bowed and one shoe about to fall off. I couldn't know the reasons why people had lied to her about her past, why she was told she had never been to Rose Point. Her mother must have had some good reason for this. Maybe Charles Halworth had met a terrible end that she never wanted her daughter to know about. Or maybe he just never loved his daughter enough to remain a part of her life. My mind settled on this possibility. All these years, right up until a few minutes ago, I had been transforming his disappearance into some epic Hollywood saga, when really he might be just another person in the world who cared only about himself.

I tried calling Billings to tell him to forget the movie, but his line was busy. I watched a red fox dash across the crusted snow and made a mental note to call him back later. I walked back to my father's shop, put the work order in his drawer, and fell asleep in his chair, wrapped in the sleeping bag.

1 2

Sometime during the night I must have laid down on the floor, because in the morning I woke with my head just a few inches from the woodstove. As soon as I opened my eyes all the confusion from the day before returned, and my mind began racing, tearing around the corners of stupid ideas and beautiful ideas, running into walls of doubt. I just lay there on the floor with everything turning to dust in my head.

I stumbled into the bathroom to pee, and then remembered the toilet wasn't working.

Outside, the whole world of Rose Point was still and frozen solid. Every standing thing—each bush and tree, each porch column and flagpole, the cottages themselves— looked like they were about to crack and fall to pieces in the snow. I turned my head slowly, taking in everything, because this morning it seemed like it had just been created for me. As I stood there, the confusion began to recede, and I said out loud, "Just be of some use here before you leave. Just do the damn work here and then go home."

Saying this, I walked to the cottage with my father's snow shovel and wearing his work boots and his blue coveralls that zipped from my right knee to just below my chin. I made tracks in the fresh snow that had fallen during the night, and when I stopped once to look back at them, I felt like I was alone for the first time in my life. Truly alone here, but not lonely, in this world that the summer people and my father no longer inhabited. It was just me now, a man with work to do.

I began to feel strong in a way I hadn't felt in years, and when I came to the cottage it was as if I were seeing it for the first time. I stood in knee-deep snow in the lane that ran along the front of the property. *Just look at this place,* I said to myself. It was magnificent. The steeply pitched roof with five matching gables. Half a dozen sleeping porches attached to turrets and decks. The elegant wraparound porch with its sky blue ceiling of matched boards. The carriage house covered in cedar shingles like the main cottage. Even though all her windows and doors were boarded up with plywood shutters painted gray, none of her beauty was diminished.

I confess that even after what my old high school classmate had said to me, even after I had renounced my idea of a movie, I could picture where the platform of lights would stand when shooting the evening scenes. I would have searched for a completely unknown actress to play Katherine as a child spending Christmas in this place where her world had fallen apart. I would have lined the porches with rocking chairs, and somewhere in the line of chairs, one small rocking chair for her miniature Olivia, as she called her. There would be a skating rink on the back lawn, and it would be on the rink where Mr. Halworth would see his daughter again for the first time in thirty years. He would take her in his arms and skate her across the ice. And what marvelous symbolism in this scene—a man who had lost everything, including himself, because of an icy road, would win it all back on the ice of a back-yard skating rink.

Just thinking about this now made me see that yesterday I had been a little crazy. Off the rails. Making a movie out of this family's misery? Maybe it was my father's death getting to me. He was gone, which meant that there wasn't anyone in the world now who cared one way or the other about what happened to me. And no one on Earth to remember me after my time was up.

I began shoveling snow at the cottage that morning, and by noon I had a portion of the porch and two brick walkways cleared. I ate a peanut-butter-and-jelly sandwich in my father's office and called my secretary.

"You missed lunch today with Elizabeth Tisdale," she reminded me. "And tomorrow there's a—"

I didn't hear the rest. "I need you to clear the decks for me for five days, Marylou."

"What should I say?" she asked.

"Tell them that my father died," I told her.

"All right," she said, and I could tell by the flatness of her voice that she accepted this as just another run-of-the-mill lie upon which more lies would be heaped until I was back in town to lie for myself.

"Marylou," I said. "It's true. My father *did* die."

She still didn't believe me. "Okay," she said. "Winfield Marshall's been calling for you every fifteen minutes all day long."

Back at the cottage, eating a second peanut-butter-and-jelly sandwich, I began sizing up the work ahead of me. Another whole day of shoveling snow, at least. Maybe a day and a half. Then taking the plywood shutters off more than seventy doors and windows, and knowing my old man, he would have put each sheet of plywood on with screws instead of nails, making it an even more time-consuming job. Then I would have to get the water and the electricity running and insulate the copper pipes beneath the house so that they wouldn't freeze. Inside, at least a whole day of cleaning. After thirty years it had to be a mess.

The telephone woke me at six the next morning. It was the man from the hardware store calling to say he hadn't been able to reach the guy he'd told me about.

"Can you tell me again?" I asked him.

"The guy at Old Orchard Beach," he said. "He owns the carousel? Used to come into the store here with your father."

I thanked him for calling, then drove into town, to fill the rental car with gas and use the men's room.

I took the Broad Turn Road out to Route 1 and headed south to Old Orchard Beach. As soon as I turned onto Ocean Drive and saw the pier I began to feel calm for the first time since I had left LA. Up ahead was the amusement park where my mother had taken me each summer on my birthday when I was a boy, the two of us holding hands in Dottie Hunter's truck while she drove us along the shore with the windows rolled down so we could hear the carnival organ from half a mile away. Our trips to the amusement park were a secret my mother and Dottie and I shared—and kept hidden from my father. You couldn't have paid him to go to an amusement park anyway, and I suppose if he'd ever found out about us going he would have just shaken his head. That wasn't the point, though; what mattered wasn't the nature of this secret I had kept with my mother, but the fact that we had kept it, that it had belonged to us and not to him. We always stopped at Crescent market on the way home and my mother bought Dottie a carton of Kool cigarettes to thank her for the ride.

As I drove along, the sounds began returning to me like something from a dream. The shrill whistle of the miniature train. The amplified voices of the midway barkers. The screeching iron wheels of the roller coaster. The nearer I got to the place, the more real these sounds became, so that when I parked on the side of the road and stepped out of the car into silence, I felt lost. The amusement park had never been more than a few ramshackle buildings nailed together, but now they were gone, and in their absence something greater seemed to have passed away.

I walked slowly through the ruins. The wooden outbuildings had fallen off their cinder-block foundations and were rotting in the wet sand. The seats had been stripped from the Ferris wheel, and all that remained was a rusted skeleton swaying in the wind. The boardwalk was in pieces. The bingo hall and souvenir shops had collapsed into the sea.

Standing in the remnants of the promenade, what I remembered suddenly was that this world with its fried dough and its fortune-tellers, its tattoo parlors and its ring-toss galleries was as far from Rose Point as the moon, and that was why my mother and I had loved it unconditionally.

I took account of all this, and then found what I was looking for. Up ahead, drowsing in the falling snow, was the low-slung, white-washed building that held the carousel. Protected by the dunes, it stood exactly as I remembered it, attached to a one-room cabin where the owner had lived. I began walking toward it slowly, remembering how my mother always tied a bandanna around her head before she climbed onto her horse with the silver stirrups. And how I always rode the horse with the cherry-colored saddle.

I was walking around the building trying to find a way to look inside when a car pulled up and a man in a Boston Celtics windbreaker got out. He waved as if he'd been expecting me, and then hollered, "You're two years too late."

I took a few steps toward him. "You're not an antique dealer?" he said.

"Not me," I said.

He was a man about seventy, I thought, with a nice smile and a wiry build. He studied me carefully, as if he were trying to decide if he could trust me. "No," he said, "you don't look anything like an antique dealer up close. Sorry."

There was something familiar about him, a warmth and a toughness that reminded me of so many older men in my hometown.

"No problem. I've been accused of far worse."

He smiled. "Same here, kid," he said. "Plenty of times."

"You look familiar," I said to him. "I used to come here as a kid years ago."

"Yeah?" he said, nodding his head. "I get visitors all the time who tell me that. But if you were a kid more than eleven years ago, it wasn't me who ran the carousel. I bought the place after I retired from the Marine Corps. You know, something to tinker with in my old age."

"I've been away a long time," I said.

"And now you're back?"

"For a little while," I said.

"Well, I bought this place off a fellow named Stintson from up in Bucksport. He bought it from one of the Kelly brothers right here in Old Orchard."

"Kelly," I said. "That's the name I remember. He had a red mustache."

"Yep. And he wore crazy silver cowboy boots, do you remember?"

"I do. Yes, I remember."

He seemed pleased. He looked at me for a few seconds, not saying anything. Then he reached into his pocket and pulled out a bunch of keys. "If you've got time, I'll let you have a look around?"

"You don't have to do that."

"I know I don't," he said.

I watched him unlock the double doors and push them back on their rails. And I know this sounds crazy, but for an instant I thought I heard the organ music starting up.

"It smells like summer," I said, as I walked inside with him. He had all the horses wrapped in burlap covers.

"*Smells* good," he said, "but I couldn't make a go of it as a business."

I told him I was sorry. "You'd think there would always be customers for a carousel," I said.

"Yeah, but some out-of-state people built a fancy place on Route 1 with water slides and go-carts. That was the end of this old fire hazard."

He looked around thoughtfully, as if he still didn't quite believe what he was telling me. "No, I couldn't compete with the dream machine video parlor across the way. Kick boxing. Shoot 'em ups. You know."

"The new world," I said.

"What about you?" he asked. "What world are you from?"

"Long ways from here," I told him. "But I grew up right in South Portland. I came here with my mom every summer as a kid."

"Is she an antique dealer?" he asked with a worried look.

"No, she's gone now," I said.

He nodded his head and asked if I wanted to see one of the horses.

"I don't want to take any more of your time," I told him.

"I've got plenty of time," he said. As he was untying the burlap bag he told me that antique dealers came by all the time offering him money for the place. "This carousel was built in 1914 by the Carousel and Taboggin Company of Willowgrove, Pennsylvania," he said. "These horses are carved from solid white oak. Take a look."

The black eyes of the white stallion with a golden mane were lifelike, and I stared into them.

"They keep me busy," he said. "Did you have a favorite horse?"

I turned and looked at him to see if he was serious.

"Most people who come by tell me they had favorites."

"Mine had a cherry-colored saddle," I said.

He pointed across the planked stage. "That one over there," he said. "A few years ago one of its front legs fell off. Had to hire a carpenter to fix it. You want to take a look?"

We knelt down in the frozen sawdust, and he explained the whole procedure to me, showing me how the carpenter had repaired the broken leg with wooden dowels. My father's work; I could tell by how perfectly it had been done. I didn't say anything to him about this. I just listened and followed him from horse to horse as he uncovered them. In the end, when he finished telling me his stories, all the burlap covers were on the ground and the carousel looked exactly as it had when I was a boy.

"We'll have some coffee together," he said.

He took hold of my arm as he turned toward the door. "Big muscle," he said, squeezing my bicep. "You an ex-marine?"

I laughed. "Not me," I said. "I work out."

"That's good. You need to stay strong. Feel this."

He flexed his arm for me.

"Amazing," I said. "How old are you anyway, thirty? Thirty-five?"

He laughed. "Times two," he said.

"Do you want me to help you cover the horses before I go?" I asked him as we neared the door.

"No, no," he said. "I'll cover them later. It'll give me something to do."

He took the padlock out of his coat pocket. "That's one of my problems now, son, I don't have enough to do. I'm still learning how to be an old man. I tell people they need to be patient with me; I was a *young* man for most of my life. This *being old* business takes some getting used to. You get my point?"

"Well, I have some work for you if you're interested," I told him. "My name's Terry McQuinn. My father was the caretaker at Rose Point. A man at the hardware store told me you two knew one another."

He looked at me with his eyes moving slowly. "My name's Warren," he said softly, and we shook hands. "Your Mac's son?"

"I am, yes."

"You said your father *was* the caretaker?"

"He died," I told him.

His eyes opened wide. He looked like he had something to say, and I waited. I didn't intend to tell him anything else; it just came out of me. "The truth is," I said, "I didn't get home in time. He died before I could see him."

I had turned away when I told him this. When I looked back at him I saw his eyes close.

He sighed, then looked at me. "That's rough," he said. His voice was low. "I'm sorry."

"Thanks," I said.

"Here's the thing, Terry," he said, surprising me by the sound of my name. "There's a lot of sadness in the world."

He waited for me to speak. "I guess you're right," I said. I thought we might go inside his cabin and talk for a while, but he seemed eager to say good-bye.

"You take care of yourself," he said, making a gesture with his hand that was part wave, part salute.

"Thanks," I said, "but would you want the work? I've got to open one of the big cottages by December twentieth."

"For a summer person?"

"Coming up for Christmas," I said.

Now he stared at me. He raised one hand and slowly traced the outline of his jaw. "Coming up for Christmas?" he said. "Why would they want to come up here for Christmas?"

"It's a long story," I said, remembering that Katherine Halworth had said the same thing to me. "I was hoping maybe you were a carpenter, too," I said.

"No," he said. "I'm sorry."

He waved again and turned away quickly. I could see that he was in a hurry as he walked toward his cabin. "Do you know anyone who could help me?" I called to him.

"Sorry," he said, without looking back at me.

I watched him go inside. I wondered if something I had said had offended him. Or if it was the mention of my father that had bothered him. Maybe he'd had a run-in with my old man. A disagreement over money, I thought. Okay, I said as I drove away, I'll do the work myself.

1 4

When I got back to Rose Point, I swore at the locked gate and walked to the shop, determined to find my father's key. I started emptying boxes and old coffee cans. I'd been at it maybe ten minutes when I cut my thumb just below the knuckle on a rusted razor blade at the back of a drawer. I thought it was nothing at first, but when I looked closely the cut was open all the way to the bone, and I knew I needed stitches.

I wrapped my hand in a rag and cursed all the way to the hospital. My second trip to the hospital in two days.

I counted twelve people ahead of me in the emergency room. All I could do was sit and wait, aware that the time I needed to work at the cottage was passing.

After a while I gave in to the waiting and just began watching people making their way in and out of the hospital through the sliding glass doors. I wish I could see things differently than I do; I mean, maybe you look at people and see the reach of history in their faces. Far away continents in their eyes. What I see are the ramifications of economics and commerce. The hospital employees with hair nets meant kitchen workers to me, people for whom life would never get easier. The men in suits were keepers of ledgers, counters of money, ambitious men looking to get somewhere. The physicians in their long white coats were the high priests of prosperity. I want to believe that someday my understanding of the world will be rooted in more spiritual ground. I can tell you this about money: Making a lot of it is not difficult if you are willing to trade away your imagination.

Someday I would also like to be a man who observes the world without turning it into an extension of myself, of my own fears and desires. Today I could think only of how I have a date with some hospital in my future as you do, a day when I will have to report in the early morning for tests that will tell me what I pretend I don't know, that I won't go on forever. When that day comes I hope I have the grace to recall how fortunate I've been to be healthy every single day of my life.

Today the hospital was doing a brisk business. The automatic doors never really closed all the way before they opened again. Did I remember these doors, how they reflected the falling snow that Christmas Eve? And if I tell you that Mr. Halworth stopped to gaze into the glass to adjust the Santa's cap on his head, am I making this up? How can we ever say with certainty what we remember from our past and what we merely invent to bridge the distance between the *then,* and the *now?*

When I think of the boy I was then and the man I have become, I know that what I have learned best across the years is how to lie. Show me a door that is locked and I will cut a lie to turn the bolt. Send the skeptic to my office and I will disarm him with the deftness of a pickpocket. Sometimes I lie when the truth would serve me just as well.

I passed out cold when they stitched up my thumb. A nice nurse was standing beside me with a glass of orange juice when I opened my eyes.

"Feeling better?" she asked.

"I have to get back to work," I told her, and I started to stand up.

"Not so fast," she said. "You get a nice ride from here. It's the rule."

She pushed me to the lobby in a wheelchair. I was surprised to see that it was already dusk. I asked her directions to the men's room, then thanked her and wished her a merry Christmas.

Inside the bathroom there was an Asian man dressed in a Santa Claus costume. He was standing at the mirror adjusting his fake beard. "Can't get it to stick on right," he complained.

The sight of him did something to me. I washed my face after he went out and then I walked back to the ER to find the nurse. I went down the glassy corridors, knowing it was a long shot.

"I was here one Christmas Eve," I said to her. "A man I knew, dressed as Santa Claus, brought gifts for the children."

She had been on the telephone about to make a call. She put the phone down, and I saw the surprise in her eyes. "You knew him?" she asked.

We stood there, neither of us moving as people hurried past us.

"He owned a cottage out at Rose Point," I said. She was nodding her head. "My father worked there."

"He came here one Christmas and there was an accident," she said. Her voice was steady and thoughtful. "And you're looking for him?"

I didn't think about what I would say next. It just came to me. "His daughter is looking for him," I told her. A small lie. Disbelief passed across her face. "It's true," I said.

"After all these years?"

"Yes."

She waited for a janitor to pass by us. Then, as if she were disclosing a great secret, she looked behind her to make sure no one else was coming. "I had a teacher at nursing school who was in love with him," she said.

1 5

Her name was Callie Boardman, and she lived in the city, only a few blocks from the nursing school at the Maine Medical Center where she had taught for more than twenty years. I was parked outside her walk-up row house on Vaughn Street, waiting for her to return home from wherever she had gone. It had begun to snow again. Every twenty minutes or so I would walk from the car to her front porch and ring her bell. Then, when the falling snow had filled my footprints, I would walk back to the porch and try the bell again.

This went on for two hours. I watched the snow mount on the roof of the building, and thought about the weight of the snow on the roof of the *Serenity* cottage. I thought of all the winter nights like this when the cottage stood alone, waiting for someone to open the doors and windows again.

She came on foot from up the street, just a woman in a long green winter coat with a pale yellow scarf around her neck. There was something solitary about the way she approached her front door, opened her purse, and took out her keys. Something solitary and completely without expectation that told me she lived alone and had for a long time.

"By choice," she said to me after she had shown me into the front room. "I've lived alone by choice. But I've had my work, you see."

I told her that I *did* see. Completely.

She knew why I was there, she said. The young nurse at the hospital had called her for me. I watched her walk into the next room and turn on a lamp. There was a table with a basket of apples sitting on a square of white linen. She began to walk back toward me, but then stopped at the table. She unwrapped her scarf and her long silver hair fell over her shoulders. She was, I thought, a woman who looked much older than her age.

After a long silence she looked up at me. "I need to catch my breath," she said. "Please sit here."

We sat across the table in straight-backed chairs, a narrow space dividing us. I could see thin red lines in her blue eyes. She offered me an apple. I smiled and thanked her. "I'm fine," I said.

She took one herself, though she only held it in her hand. "You have to wash all your fruit these days. They use far too many pesticides."

I finally took an apple, and then spoke to break the silence between us. "You've lived in the city a long time?"

She straightened her dress over her knees. "I grew up

here," she said. "It's a small city, still quite civilized, I think. I walk everywhere."

"I'd forgotten how cold it gets here," I said.

She looked at me again without saying anything more.

"I've been to the hospital," I said.

"Yes, the nurse called me."

"And now I'm here, and I don't know what to say to you."

"I think I know," she said. She folded her hands in front of her. There was a peacefulness in her eyes. "Thirty years ago, on Christmas Eve, when Charles went to the hospital with gifts for the children, his daughter was with him. And there was also a little boy. The son of the caretaker at Rose Point. He would be about your age now. He grew up and left Maine and never came back."

"Yes," I said.

"Until now."

I watched her turn the apple in her hands.

"I had a feeling we would meet someday," she said. "Why have you come home now?"

I told her that I had flown home to see my father. "But he died before I got here," I said. "I was just going to leave, to go back to California, but before my father died, Mr. Halworth's daughter called him and asked him to open the *Serenity* cottage."

She took a deep breath, tipped her head back, closed her eyes, and then opened them slowly.

"For Christmas, with her daughter," I said. "I've spoken with her, and I'm going to open the cottage for them."

"Why?" I heard her say.

"Because she asked my father to."

I said a few more things about shoveling the walkways to the cottage, but I could tell she wasn't really listening anymore. She had become distracted, or uncomfortable. I asked her if I should come back some other time. "I could come tomorrow," I said.

She turned away and walked to the chair where she had left her coat and scarf. "You have to walk with me," she said.

There are some men, many I suppose, who could turn away from a child, leaving her behind in a discarded life. But not Charles Halworth. In this respect I had been right about him all these years. As I walked through the snow with the woman who knew him best, I began finally to learn his story.

"You understand that I came to love him very much," she said. "And because of this, there are things I can't share with you, or with anyone else."

"Yes, of course," I told her.

"I met him four years after the accident," she went on, "It was almost four years."

I interrupted her without knowing why at first. "I'm sorry," I said, "but . . . I don't know what it is . . . I guess it's because all these years I've wanted to know what happened. I'm sorry, may I say something?"

I startled her, and she hesitated a moment.

"I'm sorry. I'm just feeling overwhelmed. I guess I need to tell you that I never forgot him. Or his daughter. I ran away from here, from Maine, and I kept running. It's been years. And I always told myself that I was running away from my father, because we didn't get along, we never liked each other very much. But now that I'm here, I mean standing here with you, I know I ran away because I gave up."

"Gave up what?"

I tried to find the best words. "I gave up ever seeing them again. No, not just seeing them, but being part of their life. You have to understand: My father worked for the people at Rose Point. He was never really allowed to be there. To just be there in that beautiful place. And neither was I. I was his son, of course, and no better than him. But that night, that Christmas Eve, Charles Halworth made me feel different about things. About myself. He made me feel like I was good enough. Do you see what I'm saying? I guess because I was only a kid it was possible for me to believe that his daughter and I might become friends. That I might be able to come and go in their big cottage, in a way that my father never could."

I stopped when I saw that she was smiling at me.

"What is it?" I asked her.

"It was the same thing with Charles," she said. "The big summer house, the big life, the money. None of that was his, you see. It all belonged to his wife. All he could do, he used to tell me, all he ever was good at, was skating. He grew up in Maine, in Bangor. He came from nothing. But he played hockey well enough to get a scholarship to a prep school in Boston. Then, after that, it was Harvard. That's where he met his wife. He was beautiful then. A gifted, lovely athlete. She was at Radcliffe, an attractive girl from a wealthy family. Incredibly wealthy. The kind of family you read about in magazines. Whatever they had in common, I don't know . . . youth, I suppose, turned out not to be enough. The trip to Maine that Christmas had been his idea, one last effort to try to win her back by spending Christmas at Rose Point. It's not a complicated story."

"Did he ever see his daughter again?" I asked her.

She stopped walking. Her eyes narrowed and she gazed at me. "We've just a little ways further," she said, gesturing to the hill ahead of us.

Somehow we had taken backstreets unfamiliar to me, and we ended up at the hospital. We went to a rear entrance and took an elevator to the sixth floor. The nurses there knew her by name, and they smiled and said hello and merry Christmas as we passed down the corridor.

We stopped at a small room with a glass wall. On the other side were rows of newborn babies, each in a wheeled basket with transparent sides. They all wore tiny knit hats that made them look as if they were travelers together who had taken a long journey to arrive here. One had a kind of half smile on his face as he slept. Another had managed to free one arm from the blanket and was waving it in the air like a conductor in front of an orchestra.

"I met Charles here," she told me. "It was four years after the accident. He was pushing a mop along the floor here, and when he stopped and gazed at the babies I fell in love with him . . . with whatever was in his eyes. I was very shy. Young and shy. He worked nights, and whenever I was on the late shift I would wait to see him."

She turned away and asked me to come with her. We took another elevator to the top floor. When the door opened we were in an unfinished room, a kind of storage room filled with boxes. She walked across the floor, down a narrow aisle between tall shelves, to a window.

"On a clear night like tonight you can see a long way. There's the back cove, there. And the lighthouse at Cape Elizabeth. And there, there's Rose Point."

It was amazing to me.

I told her that though my parents had told me Charles had returned after the accident, I had believed as a child that he was in trouble. "I mean, for leaving," I said. "My father told me that there were no charges against him. And I guess that's true or he wouldn't have been able to get a job here. He would have had to keep running."

She told me that my father had told me the truth. "Charles was running for a long time. Not from the police, though. He was running from himself." She paused.

"Like me."

She smiled at this. "Even when we were together, he never really stopped running," she said. "He worked here for seven years, and we were together for that time. We often stood at this window. He was always hopeful that he would see his daughter again. He was desperate to see her. And there were things he did. Well, there were some very difficult times. The police . . . You see, he spent those four years after the accident in New York City, trying to earn his way back to his daughter."

She wiped tears from her eyes, and while I waited I looked out the window. Rose Point was dark, of course, but in the summer months it would have been lit up brightly.

"I'm the one who finally convinced him to give up his hope of ever seeing Katie again," she said to me. "I was afraid it would kill him. His wife . . . his ex-wife, I hate that expression, made it impossible, and then he became desperate . . . he tried to take Katie. After that, it was over for him. But he still had this hope. I think his hope was the deepest thing inside him. A big man filled with hope. The hope of a child, really. I think that's why he loved children so much. I carry the guilt for ending his hope. As I said, I persuaded him to give up ever seeing his daughter again. I think of it every day. Because I can tell you I did this for him, but really I did it for myself. I was selfish, you see? I wanted him to live. To live for me. And in the end, I lost him anyway. I lost him to his terrible sadness."

Before I left her, we walked down State Street, to the intersection where the accident had taken place. I looked down at the slush in the street, and I heard again the sound of the baby carriage dragging beneath the car. I closed my eyes, and it all came back to me. The damp scent of the cloth seats. Mr. Halworth's arms flying up in the air. The flashing red and blue lights. A coldness ran through me as if I were standing barefoot in the snow. Then I felt her taking hold of my hand.

She looked past me in silence before she told me that in the years when Charles Halworth was with her they came here together every Christmas Eve. "Twelve years ago he disappeared from my life," she recounted. "I came alone that Christmas. I still do. It's something . . . I don't know, it's something I shouldn't do, I suppose. I should forget him. But I can't. When something terrible happens to someone you love, your friends and all the people who care about you tell you that you will get over it, in time you will get over it. To me that always seemed like the sad-dest thing, I mean, when someone you love is gone and you finally stop thinking of them. The idea that I might go through a whole day without thinking of Charles . . ."

Finally, I asked her what I should tell his daughter.

She shook her head. "Do what your heart tells you to do," she said.

"Should I tell her that her father is dead?"

She looked into my eyes. "Charles is dead. He had a brother who knew about me. He came to see me and he told me that Charles had died."

Before I left she told me that she hoped I would stop running away, and that I would find peace. I couldn't say anything. I'd grown prosperous by never showing any emotion. By never really caring too much about any of the projects I pretended to be willing to die for. And now I was crying in the street.

16

I slept again on the floor of my father's shop. If you can call it sleep. My thumb throbbed all night long. I hadn't put enough logs in the woodstove to keep it going, and I was frozen to my bones from the cold floor. Sometime in the night I got up and stood at the window. I was still standing there at daybreak, thinking how sad it was that Charles Halworth would never see the sun rise over Rose Point again. It left me feeling hollow inside, as if something precious had been taken from me.

Finally, I got the woodstove going again and, to take my mind off things, I began devising a kind of platform bed. I sketched it out on my father's workbench. Then I hauled a four-by-eight-foot sheet of ¾-inch plywood from my father's overhead rack and laid it on the table saw to cut a foot off each end. When I pushed the "on" button for the saw, nothing happened. I stood there for a few moments, staring down at it dumbly, as if I expected the blade to jump to life on its own. I felt my impatience rising, and then anger at myself when I realized that a part of me was afraid of the damned thing. I knew the awful sound that would fill the room if I ever managed to turn it on. I knew how close to the blade my right hand would come as I pushed the sheet of plywood over it. It made me think how safe my grown-up life had been. No danger. A life where I risked nothing.

Finally, I followed the electrical cord from the motor beneath the table and discovered that the saw had its own fuse box.

When the saw began whirring I got to work grimly, pushing the plywood along the metal fence, squinting into a shower of sawdust. I made the two cuts without a catastrophe. And then four more cuts to make one-foot legs from a three-by-five cedar post. I expected the frame to be steady when I screwed on the legs, somehow forgetting that I needed to connect all four legs with diagonal supports to keep it from wobbling. The whole time I worked I thought of Callie Boardman's last words to me: "Do what your heart tells you to do." I didn't know what my heart was telling me. So much sadness. This new layer of Mr. Halworth's story made it only sadder. Far better, I thought, far better if his daughter lives with only her mother's lie to stand as the truth.

When I finished making the bed I stood there and looked at it disdainfully. Here was something my old man could have made in twenty minutes. It had taken me two hours and a lot of cursing each time I lost my pencil. I had tools scattered across the floor when I was finished.

I kicked the table saw and walked away. When I looked up, my mother's face was there, her eyes staring back at me. I took the photograph in my hands and sat down with it. The rose-patterned dress. She was wearing that dress the time we went grocery shopping and I begged her for cherries. I remembered vividly how I pleaded with her to buy the cherries and how she kept telling me that they were too expensive, that my father would be angry with her for spending so much money. All I wanted was a handful, but she couldn't grant me this. And she clung to her pocketbook as if she were afraid I would try to take it from her.

Oh, God, I said, as I felt the same old anger and frustration rising inside my chest. The feeling that I was trapped in a long, dark corridor of resentment. It was something that had been a part of me for so many years, I could no longer name its point of origin. Some morning, maybe, when I'd awakened to my mother's voice calling to my father as he walked away from her? The first time he shook his fist at me? My mother at the kitchen window watching him drive away? The way he could fill a room with silence, silence that dared you to speak? Or maybe it was just his damned coldness. Put a color to that coldness and it would be the cobalt blue of the winter sky this morning. Maybe you will understand this when I tell you that I have been afraid of that coldness, afraid that it inhabits me and that I would pass it on were I to get married and have a family. I have been in love a number of times. I know the sweetness of love. There was a girl I would have married. Her name was Nicole and we were together three years, often night and day for weeks at a time. In the end she left me because I could not pass what she said was the true test of love. I could not stop thinking about myself. *My* fears, *my* desires. *My* work. *My* future. What *I* might accomplish. She made me see that the world would be better off if men as self-centered as I didn't have families. If they had the courage to live alone.

I walked across my father's shop and hung the photograph back in its place. Maybe it was the blue sky, or the sound of the shorebirds, but for once I was just plain tired of being angry over things that had happened so long ago. This was a new morning. There was a pink light out over the sea, and in the distance a small parade of fishing boats was heading out into the bay. I thought of the men on those boats, the risks and dangers they faced, and the families they were providing for.

When I opened the door and stepped outside I said to myself, This is where it stops. The anger and the resentment stop here. Right now. Kick yourself in the butt and get back to work.

But it wasn't until I had found the key to the gate and had pulled the rental car to the end of the driveway at *Serenity* cottage, opening all the doors with the radio blasting, that I began to find my way into the work. A radio station was playing the old soul music of Percy Sledge, and I was quickly caught in its rhythms. Soon I was shoveling happily to "When a Man Loves a Woman" and "Try a Little Tenderness." All the words came back to me from somewhere. Before long I was singing at the top of my lungs and shoveling to the cadence of the bass runs: "I been lovin' you, a little too long, and I can't stop now!"

When I reached the bare floor of the porch I found the boards in surprisingly good condition. Not newly painted, of course, but cared for. For this routine maintenance across the years my father must have been paid by Mrs. Halworth, I presumed, though she never returned to the place. I imagined her ambivalence as she wrote out checks for a house she no longer visited.

I looked down at my feet on the porch my father must have painted gray fifteen or twenty times in his life. Soon Mr. Halworth's daughter would walk across this porch again. She would climb the stairs I had shoveled and she would walk to the front door and push it open for the first time since she was a little girl. And now she had a little girl of her own.

I turned and looked at the mailbox by the front door. The same mailbox, painted red, with the word "POST" stenciled in white letters, just as it had been when I was eight years old and my mother brought me here to leave the piece of paper with Mr. Halworth's fingerprint.

Before I opened the lid I ran my hand over the corners, which were mitered so perfectly I knew at once that my father had built it. I could see where he had carefully caulked the seams with silicon to keep out rain and moisture. I imagined it took him an hour. Maybe a little longer. I would have been in grade school when he built it. And he would have been about the age I was now. He had used stainless steel finish nails and hinges made of bronze. "Build everything out of clear cedar, no knots in the wood, and it will last forever," he used to say. "Learn a trade and you will never go hungry."

Learn a trade. He had been preaching that to me since junior high school, and I had turned my back on his advice from day one, when I enrolled in the college prep program rather than what was called "industrial arts" in my school. I can still remember the autumn afternoons when I came out of the football locker room into the cold light and crossed the parking lot in my spiked shoes, helmet on or cocked under one arm. On my way to the practice field I passed the high school hoods from industrial arts sitting on the steps out behind the wood shop, hunched over their cigarettes, watching me with the bored, superior expression of fashion models. These were the boys in the building trades, and I looked down on them with their go-to-hell sunglasses and their motorcycle boots that they scuffed through the hallways. I was leaving them behind on the way to an exceptional life. To me they were boys who would grow up to become my father's kind of men. Hourly wage, no ambition, Lawrence Welk on Saturday nights, two weeks off a year, classic American working stiffs. As soon as I was old enough to see how the world worked, I began working hard to get enough velocity in my own life to escape my father's. Like a man fleeing a fire, I never looked back.

Until now.

Standing on the Halworths' porch it felt like all the years I was running I had been merely taking the long way home. And nothing I had done in my life, no contract with my initials on it, no commission on another person's work, seemed as substantial as the wooden mailbox my father had built in an hour, with his own hands.

When I raised the lid, I saw that there was a hole in the bottom as wide around as my thumb, and a nest in one corner. I suppose some animal had bored its way into the mailbox, and then left it for a bird to build a nest there. The nest was made from small twigs and bits of straw. When I looked closely I found a wing from a monarch butterfly, and sewn through the twigs were tiny scraps of paper that might have once been part of Mr. Halworth's fingerprint. A person with a deeper soul than my own might point out the lesson here: This creature could have claimed a twelve-bedroom house for its home, but chose instead only the space it needed in the mailbox.

I finished all the shoveling just before dark, clearing the

four brick walkways, the wraparound porches, the decks, and the driveway. In the morning I would clear the snow from the roof before the weight damaged the sheathing and rafters. Then I would begin taking the plywood shutters off the windows, doors, and the sleeping porches.

I could have started in on the roof now, in the last light of the day, but the wind had picked up and it unnerved me. I decided to wait until the next morning.

At the end of the day I took the mailbox back to the shop with me to repair the hole in the bottom board. Removing that one damaged piece without destroying the rest was not easy, and it was very late when I finally finished. I painted the bottom with oil primer and caulked the seams the way my father had, and then placed the mailbox on a stool beside the woodstove to dry.

I sat in my father's chair, listening to the wind race across the roof and rattle the loose pane of glass in the window above my head. I went through all the things I had to do at the cottage, counting and recounting the windows and doors whose shutters I would begin removing in the morning. My mind kept returning to the windows on the third floor and to the glassed-in widow's walk on the ridge of the roof. The thought of climbing that high made me acknowledge for the first time that I had become afraid of heights, though I couldn't remember when this fear began.

I ate a can of baked beans and half a pumpkin pie.

Twice, before I fell asleep, I got up to check the mailbox, opening the lid and peering inside to reassure myself that I had made the repairs well enough. In the end I set the bird's nest inside, concealing the seam so that you couldn't tell where my father's work ended and my own began. I had just turned out the light on my father's desk when I heard a car coming up the lane. I went to a window and watched as the car neared the shop. It came to a stop, and then quickly turned and drove away. I walked outside and stared into the darkness. Someone with a key to the gate, I said to myself.

1 7

I opened my eyes to sunlight and someone shaking my arm. "Wake up, Mr. McQuinn. Wake up. Rise and shine. It's me, Warren, from the carousel. You're going to freeze to death out here, kid."

I saw that he was smiling at me and shaking his head.

"The carousel?" I said.

He opened the woodstove and began stirring the coals. "You've got plenty of dry wood here," he said, turning his back to me.

"Wait," I said. "What are you doing here?"

"What am I doing here? I'm making sure you live to see sunny California again."

He was throwing every piece of wood he could reach into the fire. When he picked up the mailbox, I stopped him.

He looked at me and smiled. "It's a darn good-looking mailbox, kid, but you've got to get some heat in this place."

He set it down, finished with the woodstove, and then looked over at me, shaking his head again and breaking into a wry grin.

"Okay, I give up," I said, "but what are you doing here?"

"Bill Walters," he said.

"Who the hell's that?"

"The guy at the hardware store." He lowered his voice. "He told me you were staying out here in your father's shop. I couldn't believe it. I'm here to help you." He nodded his head solemnly.

"Your back," I said. "You told me you had a bad back."

"I can worry about my back later," he said. "First things first. Where do you want to begin?"

It took us almost two hours to get the toilet working. We had to open the main line in the pump house, which was a couple hundred yards away in the woods. Together we walked through the early morning light and the bitter cold. When we got back to the shop and opened the water taps, there was nothing.

"It's caught up somewhere underneath," he said.

We went back outside and just stood there for a second. "Can you crawl under there?" he asked. "Or should I?"

I got down on my hands and knees and then on my belly and worked my way into the crawl space under the shop floor while he knelt down in the snow and shined the flashlight. I began remembering little things my father had taught me. Wherever a copper pipe makes a turn there's an elbow with two soldered joints where water can sit and freeze. I found the first turn. The copper elbow was so cold that my fingers stuck to it.

"That looks like the place," Warren called to me.

I opened the valve on the torch, but when I put a match to it nothing happened. I tried a second time, and then a third. That's my old man, I thought: Trying to bleed every last drop of propane out of it, too cheap to buy a new cartridge of gas.

"Terry," Warren said. "You're giving it too much gas. It's blowing out the match."

He was right, of course. But then, after I got the torch lit, a gust of wind extinguished it.

"It's no use," I said. "I can't do this."

"You can," he said. "Just keep going."

I turned and saw his knees in the snow. "You must have better things to do than this," I said sarcastically.

"I do, but then where would *you* be? Try it again."

I propped myself on one elbow to block the wind. I struck the match against the head of a nail in the floor joist above my left shoulder and the flame turned to a steady blue streak.

I put plenty of heat on the first elbow, waiting for the sound of water rushing through the pipe, but there was nothing. I slid along the ground to the next turn. For some reason my mind went out to the West Coast, and I thought of Bill Riley in the office next to mine. The silent competition between us over who had the better inventory of suits. On Saturdays we'd get together sometimes, dressed in our best suits, to sit and watch golf on TV at his place. He'd hire a cocktail waitress he liked from the Forman's Club to serve us in his den.

"I'll just keep talking until you tell me to shut my trap," I heard Warren say. He began telling me how badly he had missed the cold weather during the war when he was stationed in the Philippines with the marines. "I made a promise that if I ever got back to Maine in one piece, I'd never curse the cold again," he said.

It was later, after he and I had filled my father's shop with cigar smoke to celebrate the small miracle of a flushing toilet, that I remembered how, yesterday at the carousel, after I'd told him who I was and that my father had died, he had suddenly seemed eager for me to leave. Now he was in no hurry. He brought up the war again and leaned back in his chair, as if he would stay all day.

He told me that he had awakened every morning of his life in his father's house until he joined the marines at the age of eighteen. "I got to the Pacific and I was so scared my first few weeks that I brushed my teeth forty or fifty times a day just because it was the only normal thing I could do there in that strange place. It calmed me."

I watched him bow his head a moment. "I'll tell you what the war taught me though, son," he said. "To appreciate the little things. The smell of coffee. A friend beside you. The chance to sit and talk like we are this morning."

"That's nice, Warren," I said. "And for helping me here, I want to pay you."

"That's silly," he said. "Anyway, I still owe your father for a job he did on one of my horses. Like I said, I was out of town all last week." He shook his head. "I never got the chance to pay him."

"Well, your time is valuable," I said.

He waved this idea aside. "I've got too much time, already told you that."

"Nope," I said, "no one has too much time. I wonder how many bathrooms the cottage has."

"Six," he said, nodding his head.

I looked at him for a second. "You know?"

"No, no, no, I'm just guessing six, at least. Every place out here must have at least a half dozen bathrooms. Big parties going on all the time and everything."

"Yeah, I guess so," I said. I was trying to remember if I'd told him yesterday at the carousel which cottage I was opening for Christmas. "Have you ever spent any time out here, Warren?" I asked him.

"Here?" he said, raising his hands in the air to dismiss the very notion. "Three or four times with your father, that's all," he said. "I don't know as an old marine would find too many friends out here. Out-of-state people, you know what I mean? And as for you, kid, you need some decent boots or you'll go back to California with your toes frozen off."

"I'll get some," I said. "Is there anybody around here who might have a key to the gate?" I stared right into his eyes.

"This gate?" he said.

"Yeah. Do you know if my father ever gave anybody a key to this gate?"

"I wouldn't know, son," he said.

I watched him sit up straight. *Nervous,* I thought.

"Someone drove in here last night," I said. "Now that I think of it though, I probably left the gate open."

"I'm forgetting things all the time," he said, shaking his head.

"Where'd you park?" I asked him.

"Park?" he said.

I had him, and I knew it. "This morning," I said.

"Oh," he said. "You confused me. Outside the gate. It was locked when I drove up."

"Locked," I said. "So I didn't leave it open last night? That's a mystery, I guess. Like life itself, right?"

"Right you are, son," he said, with relief. "You want to start opening up that cottage?"

18

If you lie to people long enough you know when you're being lied to, and you learn a kind of patience with liars, knowing that if you give them enough time, their lies will lead you to the truth they are trying to conceal. For this reason alone I might have decided not to challenge Warren. I had another reason as well. I needed his help to open the cottage.

This morning, as we walked toward *Serenity*, he walked behind me.

"Here she is," I said, when we were standing in front of the cottage. He tipped his head back in the early morning light. I watched as he clasped his hands in front of him. For a moment I thought he might be praying, and I felt like an intruder.

"Imagine," he said, softly, almost as if he were talking to himself. "Imagine living in such a beautiful house."

"I hate to ask you this, Warren," I said, "but could you hold the ladder for me while I take off the shutters on the second and third floors. The truth is, I'm afraid of heights."

"You want me to climb up?" he asked, eagerly. "I don't mind at all. Heck, you know, I didn't mention this before, but if you've got to get back to California, just go. There's nothing here I can't do by myself. And I've got time. You can just write me out a list of things you want done, son, and I'll have the place opened for you."

I smiled at him. "You don't want to get rid of me do you?" I said, with a laugh to make it easier for him to deny.

"It's not that," he said.

"I know it isn't, I'm only kidding. Why would you want to get rid of me?" He looked away nervously.

"I'll tell you something," I began. "You're probably right, I ought to hire you to open this cottage, and I should head back home. But something tells me that this is where I belong right now. Does that make any sense?"

I may have disappointed him, but he did not oppose me. "Well, then," he said, "let's get to work."

We opened the widow's walk first, and from the top rung of my ladder I could see the outline of the hospital far off across the cove. It was snowing again, big fat flakes swirling slowly through the gray sky. I was afraid to look down to watch them land. Warren was below, holding the ladder.

My father had fastened the shutters across each window with galvanized screws. I used a cordless drill with a

Phillips-head bit, and worked slowly, trying to take deep, even breaths, and always holding onto something with my free hand. When I uncovered the first window, I heard Warren call up to me: "You want to switch places?"

"It's okay," I called back to him. One window and then the next. Like taking the coins off a dead man's eyes. It wasn't until I had all eight windows uncovered on the widow's walk that I leaned close to the glass and looked inside. The center of the floor was open to a set of stairs that ran down through the ceiling of the third floor below, just as I remembered. There was the most elaborate set of cobwebs reaching from the tops of the windows to the sills. The bodies of dead flies and moths were trapped there, their wings and heads had been eaten away, only the shells of their torsos remained. In one corner of the room I saw a Christmas tree stand, its metal legs painted bright green. Beside it lay strands of lights, seven strands in all, each neatly coiled along one wall. My father's work, I could tell. Finally, I saw the angel in a white box on the floor. As I looked inside I remembered decorating the tree with my father and him letting me stand on a chair to put on the angel. She had a tiny lightbulb on her back that illuminated her gauze wings. Though I had never recalled this before, looking in the widow's walk brought back the memory so vividly that it might have originated in a recent day and not the distant past.

I came down the ladder one rung at a time, with my

eyes closed. "Warren," I said when I reached the ground, "can you believe my father put caulking on each shutter to keep out the dampness? I expected the house would be crumbling inside, but it's going to be in perfect condition."

"That's something," he said.

I saw that his lips were blue with cold, a cold that I had forgotten as I worked.

"Let's go warm up in the shop," I said.

"I'd like to," he said, "but I have to be home before noon."

"Sure," I said.

"Don't try to get the high windows until I'm here tomorrow to hold the ladder for you," he said.

"I'll leave the gate open for you," I told him. I looked into his eyes for something.

"Right," he said, nodding his head.

I promised him I wouldn't try to do the rest of the shutters myself and we shook hands on this.

I spent the afternoon on my back beneath the cottage wrapping heat tapes around the water pipes until it grew too dark to see. And that night before I slept I drove back into the city and parked in front of Callie's apartment. I don't know why. I guess it was just that we had shared something. I thought how fortunate Charles Halworth had been to find her after his life fell apart, and I wondered why he ever let her go.

I watched her lights go on and off that night. Only one room lit at a time, which tells a great deal about what it's like to be alone in the world. First her kitchen light, where I imagined she fixed herself something for dinner. Then that light went out, and her dining room light went on as she ate her meal. Finally, the kitchen light was on again, as she cleaned up. And at last the light in her bedroom. I had no way of knowing, of course, what it was she thought about all these years just before she fell asleep at night. But I was quite sure that this night was different, now that she knew Charles Halworth's daughter was returning to Maine.

I couldn't help walking back to *Serenity* that night before I slept. Looking up at the windows from the front lawn, seeing the moonlight reflected off the glass now that the shutters were gone, I began to feel that I was drawing near to all I might yet know.

19

I was already working at the cottage when Warren showed up early the next morning.

"Hey, you weren't supposed to go that high alone," he yelled to me.

"Couldn't help it," I called down. "I want to get off all these shutters so I can have a look inside."

He started walking toward me. "All right then," he said. "I'm still here with you."

The sky was overcast all morning and the temperature never got above the single numbers. We pulled off thirty shutters and then stopped for lunch. I climbed down and told Warren that by this time tomorrow we would be inside the cottage.

"I want to get inside, don't you?" I said to him.

"You're the chief engineer," he said.

While we ate our sandwiches on the porch the sun broke through, and the lawns and open fields for as far as you could see looked like they were covered with splinters of glass. Warren had a far-off look in his eyes. Then he began talking about the war again.

"By the time Vietnam came around," he said, "the corps wouldn't let me see combat. Stuck me in a desk job. The worst duty I ever pulled. This one other poor sod and I had to write letters home to mothers. Not for the dead marines, but for the wounded ones."

He stopped for a moment, then went on.

"A man goes off to war and he figures the worst thing that can happen to him is he gets killed. But I'll say this now, Terry, dying isn't the worst thing that can happen to you. Some of those boys were shot up so bad. I mean, some medic in the field just stuffed them back together as best he could. Then I got to write the letter to the boy's mother or wife telling her that the boy she loved would be on his way home soon. Times it would have been more compassionate to just list the boys as dead, the shape they were in."

I waited until he was finished talking. He stood up and looked out across the water. "Did my father ever tell you anything about this cottage?" I asked him. "About what happened here a long time ago?"

"No," he said. "I only saw your dad here and there and that was to drop off my horses that needed to be repaired. Dry rot, you know. He was a fine carpenter."

While we worked that afternoon I told him everything I knew about Charles Halworth and Callie, and Charles's daughter. He was curious enough to ask me questions. "The thing I don't understand is why the daughter would want to come back now," he said.

"She seems like she's got quite a spirit," I said. "On the telephone, at least. I guess she might just want to see what it is she's inherited up here."

He asked me if I was married. "Never been," I said.

"Twice for me," he said. "Both died. Both wonderful ladies. It was my last wife who convinced me that we should give our customers extra time on each ride. She read somewhere that the average length of a carousel ride in this country was seven minutes. We went up to nine from then on. People were pleased, I think. But it didn't save us."

"Well," I said, "sometimes you do the right thing just because it's the right thing to do, right?"

"That's the truth, son," he said.

We talked a while about Hollywood. He told me that he watched the Academy Awards every year. "I used to be able to tell you who won such and such an award going back pretty far," he said. "But I've lost track now."

"Watch this year, and I'll wave to you, Warren," I said.

He laughed at this.

As we opened more and more windows that day the inside of the house filled with light, and I had a sense of a life interrupted as if by a sudden turn in the wind. A reversal of fortune.

By dusk we had finished all but the front door. "We're going in together," I said to Warren. As soon as I took out the first screw I knew that they had been removed recently. The caulking had been cracked and the screws came out too easily. And when I looked through the glass panel on the door I saw snow on the floor of the foyer.

"Snow on the floor," I said to Warren.

"Blown in under the door, probably," he said.

I pushed the door open. You could see plain as day that the snow had fallen off someone's boots.

"Look at this footprint," I said.

I knelt down. Warren was standing behind me.

"Who would have been in here?" I said. I turned and looked at him. He shrugged his shoulders.

I stood up and walked ahead, glancing into the big room on my left. "I suppose my father might have come inside," I said. "I mean, he could have come in and looked around after he got the call to open the place. Right?" I turned and looked back at Warren again.

"To tell you the truth, I don't feel comfortable," he said. "I mean, walking in here, in somebody else's house."

"It's all right," I said. "Let's find the fuse box so we can see where we're going."

We found the door to the basement and went down together. The main switch was on a wall across from the stairs. "You do the honors, Warren," I said.

"No, they're your honors," he said.

An overhead bulb lit up above our heads when I threw the switch. We both turned and looked at it at the same time. Then, to the right, where there was a laundry room with a washer and a dryer and a long slate sink. To the left, a giant room with shelves built on every wall, from floor to ceiling, all of them completely empty.

On the first floor it was the same. Empty. A kind of emptiness I had never seen or felt before. The furniture was still there, all of it arranged neatly, but there was nothing personal in any of the rooms. Nothing, not even a book in the walnut-paneled library. A book which might have given some clue about the person who had read it.

"Strange," I heard myself say.

"Well, it's been a lot of years, right?" Warren said.

"I've been in empty houses before after someone you know moves away. There are always traces of them left behind," I said. "Don't you think?"

On the second floor the mattresses on the beds were covered with sheets of newspaper. I leaned over a picture of Lee Harvey Oswald. On the bed in the room across the hall, pictures of Jack Ruby and Jackie Kennedy. Newspapers my father used in December of 1963 when he closed the cottage. I counted sixteen beds in the twelve bedrooms, all of the mattresses covered by similar photographs. The funeral procession. The White House. The Kennedy compound at Hyannisport.

The mahogany wood stairways had ornate banisters.

There were oriental rugs on the floors. In one living room, a wrought-iron glider from the porch, its cushions covered in deep blue material with gold piping. It was like a museum, or the set of some summer stock theater that had been closed down short of its running time—by bad reviews.

In eighteen rooms the most personal thing I came across was a shoe-shine kit. "Look at this," I said to Warren. The kit had two tins of polish, black and brown. Only the black had been opened, and I thought at once of Mr. Halworth's black Santa boots. And his daughter's black patent leather shoes.

We were on our way downstairs when I opened what I thought was a closet door. Inside was a narrow set of stairs with snow on them and more boot prints. "My father was here," I said, "I'm sure of it."

We followed the stairs to a room hidden behind the kitchen. On one wall there was a panel of bells. "Maids' quarters," I said. "Look at this, Warren."

I found the old wiring still connected.

"Excuse me for a minute," he said. "I'll be right back."

I heard him leave, and when I turned around I saw a white bureau with some things set on top. The first sign of life in the cottage.

A pair of leather slippers. Gold-framed glasses. An appointment book with the year 1964 printed in gold on the front cover above the Brooks Brothers logo. When I opened it I saw Charles Halworth's signature. I turned the pages, slowly at first, and then hurriedly. They were all empty except for a notation on July 7, printed in black ink. "Katherine's sixth birthday."

When I opened the top drawer there were framed photographs of Charles Halworth and his daughter. The two of them in a sailboat with the child at the tiller. A young Charles in a hockey uniform leaning against the goal on some rink. Katherine as an infant asleep on a couch with a dog sleeping next to her. Katherine and her father holding croquet mallets.

The other three drawers were empty, though I checked them twice, hoping to find something. I don't know how long I stayed there before I followed the narrow stairs down to the kitchen. Warren was standing at the sink, looking out the window.

"What do you think, chief?" he said, when he heard me.

"There are some things upstairs," I said. "Sad. They made me sad, Warren . . . I feel like taking a break. Will you have dinner and a couple of beers with me?"

He turned and we looked at each other. "A man shouldn't drink by himself," he said.

"I can pick up some Chinese, if you want? Or burgers?"

"Either one for me," Warren said.

"Okay," I said. "Give me half an hour. We'll eat and drink and start in on the plumbing. Is that all right?"

2 0

As soon as I drove away, my cellphone rang. Twice. Three times. The office, I thought. I almost didn't answer it.

"Mr. McQuinn, is that you?"

When I heard Katherine's voice I felt relieved that I no longer had any designs for making a movie of her life. Making a movie would have meant that I wanted something from her, something I wouldn't stop at *anything* to get. Now, instead, I could just listen to her voice tonight, delighting in it as if I were listening to music.

"And how are you, Mr. McQuinn?" she asked.

"Call me Terry," I said.

"Thank you, Terry."

"I'm fine," I said. "Doing well. And you?"

"Excited," she said. "Olivia and I are getting more and more excited each day. We'll probably drive you crazy when we get there."

I smiled and wondered what it would be like for her when I showed her the photographs of her and her father. I would have to tell her as soon as they arrived, and then go up the hidden stairway with her to stand beside her.

"Well, here's a silly question, she said. "I'm just wondering if we should bring linens. Sheets and towels. Blankets."

I told her that I hadn't come upon any in the cottage so far.

"So you've been inside?"

"Just finished taking off the shutters. Then I went inside."

"How is it?"

"Empty," I said.

"We'd better bring linens. Olivia and I have been talking nonstop about all the things we're going to do when we get there. Tell me, is there anything we can bring for you? From New York, I mean."

"From New York City?"

"Yes."

"I really can't think of anything I need," I told her.

"Well, you don't have to *need* it. How about something you don't need at all?"

"Something I don't need?"

"Yes. Maybe one of those little paperweights of the Statue of Liberty?"

"That's great," I said. "I don't need a paperweight."

"Now you've got the idea," she said. She thanked me again for all my work.

"You're welcome," I said.

"I've been telling Olivia that our first day in Maine is

going to become our best 'live-over' day. It's a thing she and I do together. Pretend that we're going to have the chance to live over the best days we ever had. Live-over days. You only get five, so you have to choose carefully."

I was trying to decide on my own live-over days while I waited in line at Burger King. I still didn't have one when I stopped at the hardware store for insulation to cover the water pump and the hot-water heater. I had just stepped inside when the owner called to me: "Hey, how are things at the cottage? Did Warren Halworth ever stop by to help you?"

I turned and looked at him. For a few seconds there was a loud rushing noise in my head that silenced everything around me and I couldn't speak.

"What did you say?" I asked at last.

"You know, the old-timer I told you about? From the carousel?"

21

We pass over continents of time in our lives, moving weightlessly the way we move in our dreams, crossing the borders of silent moments that change us forever so that we can never cross back to where and who we once were. I haven't always believed this, but now it is one of the few things that I hold to firmly.

I raced back to the point, rehearsing how I was going to question Warren, shifting the sentences in my mind and trying to find my anger. When I got to the cottage, he was gone. The lights were on, but there was no sign of him. He knew that I had gone to town for our dinner; I was sure there was no misunderstanding about that. I checked the shop, thinking perhaps he was waiting for me there, but the lights were off.

I found him at the carousel. He had taken the canvas hoods off all of the horses, and I watched for a few moments while he went from one to the next with a cloth in his hand, cleaning them.

I stood in the open doorway with the dark winter sky behind me. I could see his breath rising above him. "Tell me who you are," I called to him. I was surprised that my voice was even and low. I felt only a strange kind of disappointment. Like something I never quite touched had been taken from me.

He wouldn't turn and look at me. "And while you're at it," I said, "tell me who gave you a key to the gate."

"I'm a bad liar," he said. "Always was."

"I'll wait right here, then, for the truth," I said.

He turned slowly and faced me. He was folding the rag in his hands. Folding and unfolding it. "I wish you hadn't come home from California," he said. Then he shook his head and dropped his hands to his sides. "No offense to you. I don't mean to hurt you in any way. But this isn't easy for anybody."

"What isn't easy?"

He thought a moment. "The truth," he said. "Those things in the bureau, your father never told you about them?"

"We never talked."

"I saw them in his shop the first time I met your dad," he said in slow, measured words. "Mrs. Halworth hired people to clean out the cottage a long time ago. Your father got in there ahead of them and saved those few things. When he showed them to me, he said—and I'll never forget him saying this—'Nobody should ever be completely forgotten.' When he told me the week before last that Katherine had called and was coming up, he said he was going to put the things back in the cottage for her to find."

Warren stopped and looked at the ground a moment. When he looked up at me he told me that he and my father had had a disagreement over this. "I told him I thought it was best if she never found out anything about her father. Your dad felt different. He told me he was going to put the things back in the cottage, and then he gave me a key to the gate, and another, I've got it right here, for the back-door. He told me that if I wanted the things gone, then I could come and take them. But he was putting them back where he'd found them thirty years ago." He turned his head and smiled a half smile. "Your father went by the book, son. But I guess you already know that."

"I guess I know it as well as anyone," I said, with a touch of scorn in my voice.

"You shouldn't be so hard on him," he said. "Fathers make mistakes."

"Sometimes they abandon their children," I said.

I saw a look of shock cross his face, but it instantly transformed itself into something else. "Terry," he said, the way a patient father would speak to a child, "you've got it all wrong."

Then I stared hard at him. I wanted an honest answer to a thirty-year-old question. "Tell me what really happened."

He looked away from me, and I thought he might not answer this. "You'll have to come with me so I can show you," he said.

22

I didn't ask him where we were going. We drove into the city. He turned onto Congress Street and drove slowly, passing the statue of the poet Longfellow in Monument Square, where a tall blue spruce tree had been decorated for Christmas. The center of the city was bustling with shoppers wearing hats and mittens and carrying brightly wrapped packages. They reminded me that it was Christmas; somehow I'd forgotten again.

In front of the library a small Salvation Army band was playing carols. The brass horns glistened like gold in the light of the overhanging street lamps. The shop windows were decorated for the season and on every corner; colored lights and lit-up wreaths hung from the street signs.

"Maybe I was wrong before. Maybe I'm glad you came home," Warren said to me, as he turned into a parking garage on Exchange Street. He stopped at a lighted booth, where a man with a flashing candy cane tie clasp handed him a ticket.

"How are you, Phil?" Warren asked.

"I'm holding my own," he replied. "Freezing cold. This is a good night for it."

"It is," Warren said.

We drove through a labyrinth of ramps and concrete columns until we reached one of the top floors and parked in a far corner. Warren kept the motor running. He checked his watch. "The symphony starts in twenty minutes," he said.

"A good night for what?" I asked him.

"You'll see, son," he said. Then he changed the subject. "Isn't she a lovely woman?" He asked. "In my long life I've never met anyone like Callie Boardman. Imagine you coming home and meeting both of us." He reached into the glove compartment and took out a deck of cards. "I used to go out to Rose Point every Thursday morning in the winter to play cribbage with your dad, and to talk."

"I don't remember him as much of a talker," I said.

"It wasn't until after your mother passed away that he opened up. But once he started talking, he seemed to like it. Your mother and I shared the same birthday; I don't suppose he ever told you that."

"No."

"You're still angry at him?"

"I don't think so," I said.

He looked at me. "He understood better than most people, I think, because he came from nothing. There he was with the keys to paradise at Rose Point. All those wealthy people surrounding him."

"Understood what?" I asked him.

I don't think he heard me. "The last time I played cards with your father I looked up from dealing a hand and he was staring at the walls of the shop. Not just staring, but turning his head slowly, taking everything in. It was as if he knew that he wasn't going to be there much longer and he wanted to remember everything."

Neither of us spoke for a moment. "You said he understood. Understood what?" I asked him again.

"Understood Charles. I think he understood him better than I did. To me, though he was twelve years younger, I idolized him growing up. He had everything. He looked like a movie star. When we'd walk into a restaurant together, the waitresses would stop working and just stare at him. And it wasn't just ice hockey that he was good at. He turned down a baseball scholarship, too. Colleges from all over the country. Coaches would come all the way to Bangor, Maine, just to take him out to lunch. I knew I wasn't ever going to leave Maine, there wasn't anything special about me. But Charles had the whole world just waiting for him. Harvard . . . I went down to see him there. I saw him play half a dozen times. Then came the Olympics. Her father or grandfather was on some important committee that picked the athletes, that's how they met."

He paused and took a knit hat from under the seat and put it on. "But he was a simple man at heart. What he wanted to do with his life was be a carpenter like your dad. That's true. He was a happy man with a hammer in his hand. But a carpenter wasn't what his wife had in mind for him. For a while she tried to make him into something, a stockbroker or some such thing. He didn't have the heart for it. He was a guy who never knew where his pants were in the morning, and money to him was only paper." He laughed a nervous laugh and told me that Charles hated neckties. "Positively despised them. His wife kept buying him these silk ties from England. When he had enough of them, a whole closet full, he had them sewn together to make a flag that he flew at the yacht club one summer." He laughed at this.

"Cocktail parties were like a prison sentence, he always told me. I remember him dragging me to a few at Rose Point. We'd sneak off and shoot basketballs behind the carriage house. I saw his wife go into a rage once when she caught us leaving through the backdoor. You'd have thought she'd caught him with his arms around another woman. No, I guess I knew from the start that it wasn't going to work between them. Charles tried to talk her out of marrying him in the first place. Then he put me up to trying to talk her out of it. I was the best man at the wedding. In her eyes, though, I was the worst man. She never liked me. Much too common. Even in a tuxedo. My mother used to say, 'You can't make a silk purse out of a pig's ear.' That's me. To Charles's wife I was nothing but a Maine hick who reminded her that her husband was the same thing at heart. Scratch off the paint and you find the wood has knots in it."

He stopped suddenly and sat up straight. I watched him point over the dashboard. "It's almost time for the music to begin," he said.

He checked his watch again. I noticed a steady stream of cars had begun pulling into the garage—a procession of Mercedes, Volvos, and the occasional Lexus. "Just like you have in Hollywood, I bet," he said to me. "The symphony should thank God for doctors."

The men and women getting out of these automobiles were dressed in evening gowns and long cashmere overcoats. I could hear the womens' heels on the concrete as they hurried into elevators and disappeared.

Another few minutes passed before the garage was silent again.

"Here they come," Warren said, just above a whisper.

I never see homeless people without thinking of the brilliant movie *Ironweed*. Tonight was no exception. But in my life I only drive past the homeless, and so I was unprepared for what I saw next. Each man and woman in rags took a different car and spread out on the hood of the engine.

"What are they doing?" I asked Warren.

"Keeping warm," he said. "On a cold night like this, they go from one parking garage to the next."

While we watched I counted thirteen men and women. Most of them laying with their arms out at their sides, as if they were trying to embrace the cars. "I think of them as fallen angels," Warren said, softly. "When they lay like that, I mean."

"It's like they're asleep," I said.

"Sometimes they *will* fall asleep," he said. "You know I bought the carousel so I could be near him."

He was distracted then, and I watched him as his eyes moved from one car to the next. Finally, he nodded. "This is the hard part," he said. He turned and looked at me. Then he pointed to a man lying across the hood of a silver station wagon. "There," he said. "There's my brother."

He had a gray beard, and a rag of what must have once been a beautiful navy blue coat that reached almost to his ankles.

"That's Charles?" I said. "He's your brother?"

Warren reached in front of me and rolled down my window. "It's up to you," he said. "Maybe I'm wrong. Call his name if you want. Leave those things in the cottage. Do whatever you think is right. But you have to promise me one thing. You won't tell Callie. She believes he's dead. And there are things worse than that, remember?"

2 3

I drank too much scotch that night, staring at the telephone on my father's desk, trying to get up the courage to call Katherine to tell her. *To tell her what?* That I had to leave before she arrived? Yes, that was it. There were a hundred excuses, a thousand small lies I could tell her so that I wouldn't be here pretending I didn't know anything. Even *I* wasn't a good enough actor to pull off that deceit.

I thought about what Warren had told me, the things my father had done here after Katherine called him to open *Serenity.* He had gone into the cottage with the photographs and the date book, the things he had saved for thirty years, trying to reinstate Charles and Katherine in the cottage where they had last been happy in one another's presence.

It was an old rotary telephone on my father's desk and I dialed Katherine's number over and over with the phone on the hook until I could repeat the numbers without looking at them. Numbers my father had written down with a steady hand.

As soon as I heard her voice on the line I apologized. "It's late," I said. "I'm sorry."

She told me it was all right, that she was up anyway. "I'm reading to Olivia," she said. "Is it snowing there?"

I could see only my own reflection in the dark windows. "I'm not sure," I said. "I'm sitting here in my father's shop, but you don't know where that is, do you? And you never met my father, did you?"

"Are you all right?" she asked.

"And you never met me, Katherine. I'm just a voice on this telephone wire, if it is wire that they use. I'm sorry. I figured out about an hour ago that I am exactly thirty-eight years, seven months, and four days old. I've been on the planet that long anyway, and I am trying to calculate what my father was doing at exactly this same age. Have you ever done that? I mean, have you ever looked at your mother and wondered if you had done the right things with your life? I'm sorry, you don't have to answer that question. It's a preposterous question. Stupid. I've been drinking. But there was this magazine in my father's desk, here in his shop? His shop is on the golf course at the point. Did you know there was a golf course?"

"No," she said. "But the golf course must be under snow by now?"

"Yes. Lots of snow here. There's this article, though, I just read this article about the invasion of Normandy. I don't know why my father kept it. It was on a shelf beside his band saw covered with sawdust and wood shavings. A picture of Eisenhower speaking to a group of paratroopers the night before the invasion, just before they got into their airplanes. They're boys, Katherine. Their faces are so young. Eighteen. Nineteen years old, and it says that they had been told that eighty percent of them would be dead before morning. Did you know that? Eighty percent. I'll let you go. I'm sorry."

"No," she said. "Don't go."

Don't go, I said to myself.

"Yes, here I am," she said, "I'm listening."

"Beep. Beep. That's for your little daughter."

"Thank you, yes. What were you going to tell me?"

"I don't know."

"About the magazine?"

"Yes. There isn't any fear on their faces, though. They are about to die and they're so courageous. I don't know if I have any courage at all. I've never been tested. I mean, my life is very safe."

"Safe?"

"I've been drinking."

"I think I could tell."

"I don't often drink."

"Well, that's probably good."

"There must be a lot of homeless people in New York."

"Yes."

"Did you see the movie, *Ironweed?* Years ago?"

"Oh yes. I loved that movie."

"You did? I did, too. I loved it."

"Meryl Streep," she said. "Jack Nicolson. And who played his mother?"

"Odelle Bowman."

"She was extraordinary."

"It's late to be talking about movies," I said. "I'm sorry."

"Don't apologize again," she said.

"I won't. I'm sorry."

"You did it again."

I heard her laugh. "Did what?"

"If I tell you, you'll only do it again," she said, laughing more heartily now. "Mommy is talking to a very silly man," I heard her say to her daughter.

"Katherine," I said.

"Yes?"

"I have to let go of you, Katherine."

"Let go of me?"

"I mean, let you go. I have to let you go because it's late and the only reason you're awake is because some idiot called you from Maine."

"We're leaving on Thursday."

"Where are you going?"

"To Maine, where you are now."

"Oh, yes, of course. To Rose Point. You're coming Thursday. Day after tomorrow. Yes, that's why I called you. I wanted to tell you that I can't be here when you arrive."

"You're leaving?"

"Yes. I can't be here this time at all. I have to go back to California."

"Oh," she said. "I'm sorry."

"You don't have to apologize," I said. "It's time for me to go home, that's all."

Her voice was just a whisper when she thanked me for everything I had done.

"So you're flying to LA?"

"Yes."

"From Boston?"

"Yes."

"Well then," she said, "maybe we won't come to Maine. Maybe we'll wait until some other time."

"No, you should come. Everything is ready for you," I said.

"I want you to send me a bill for your time," she said.

"No, that's silly."

"I insist," she said. "In case we don't come to Maine, I want you to write down my address and send me a bill."

I wrote it down. "Where will you go if you don't come here for Christmas?"

"Oh, someplace warm, I guess."

She said that she hoped we would meet someday. And this lingered with me while I slept in my father's chair with my head down on his desk.

24

At first light a throbbing pain in my head woke me. Above my eyes my skull felt like it was splitting. I drank two mugs of instant coffee and went back to work.

Halfway through the morning someone shouted at me over the sound of the vacuum cleaner I was running across the tile-floored foyer of the cottage. I couldn't tell you the last time I had used a vacuum cleaner. I'd been at it for an hour, stopping every ten minutes to curse the hose, which kept twisting itself into knots. The temperature was in the teens outside, but I had all the windows and doors wide open to air the place out. I don't know how long he had been standing behind me, yelling. When I heard him, I turned and looked into the face of a tall, lanky kid who was breathing hard. He couldn't have been more than twenty years old, a boy really.

"They told me some old guy would meet me at the gate. I waited an hour."

"What are you talking about?"

"The tree," he said. "The Christmas tree. There was supposed to be a guy to meet me at the gate. I've been walking around in circles out here for two hours freezing my tail off."

"Do you have a name? The old guy's name?"

"McQuinn. Something McQuinn," he said.

"That would have been my father. I'm sorry, kid. He died a few days ago."

His face turned red. "Oh Jeeze," he said.

"No, never mind," I told him. "What's this about a tree?"

"I carried it for a while," he said, making a half turn and gesturing behind him. "I tried not to drag it too much. What do you want me to do now?"

We drove back down Winslow Homer Lane in my car. I made him sit for a while so the heater could warm him.

"How long have you been in this business?" I asked him.

"Trees? It's my father's tree farm. I was in college but I left."

"Where?" I asked him.

"Colgate university. Like the toothpaste?"

"I know Colgate," I told him. "Upstate New York. I played against them in football, once. Just a scrimmage. Why'd you leave?"

"Why'd I leave? It was a silly school. Lazy professors. I didn't like it there. And my dad needed me."

I liked the kid. "I hope your old man appreciates that."

"I guess he does. I've got to get going, though; he's

going to chew me out for this. I should have been back an hour ago."

"Give me his number; I'll call and tell him it was my fault."

"No, that's all right."

"Well, do you have a bill?"

He went to his truck and came back with an invoice that had the name and number of the tree farm in Waterville, Maine, about two hours north of Rose Point. The tree cost forty-seven dollars. Stapled to the back of the invoice was my father's check.

He followed in the truck. I knew where my father had planned to put the tree. As we passed through the rooms of the cottage I saw him looking around at everything. "I've never seen a house like this before," he said.

Together we got the tree into the metal stand. It fit the room perfectly.

"Enough room on top for an angel," the kid said.

I told him that my father was a man who would have made his measurements carefully. "'Measure twice, cut once,' was a motto he lived by," I told him.

Sunlight broke through the gray sky while we were standing there, lighting up the red and green channel markers in the bay.

"This is an amazing place," he said, as he turned slowly, taking it all in.

"You can see the city from here," I said. "That tall

building is the hospital. On a clear day you can see all the way to Mount Washington in the west there."

"And you work here?" he said.

"No, I'm just finishing up a job for my father."

"Who owns the place anyway?" he asked.

"A woman from New York City."

"Figures," he said.

I heard myself in that remark. "You'd like her," I said to him.

I spent so much time vacuuming and mopping the first-floor rooms that by the time I returned from town late that afternoon with the plastic tarp and the lumber to build the skating rink, I had to use the car's headlights to see what I was doing. And the whole time I worked on it I thought about my father going to the trouble of ordering a Christmas tree for Charles Halworth's daughter. In his shop I had matched the date of the invoice with the date on the work order. He had ordered the tree for Mr. Halworth's daughter the day she told him she was coming to the cottage for Christmas.

Warren met me at *Serenity* to help put down the ice rink. We shoveled the snow off a twenty-by-twenty-foot square of the yard beside the kitchen, then drove two-by-fours into the frozen ground around the perimeter to hold in the water. The stars overhead were low and bright, so bright that they seemed to be moving as you stared at them. I told Warren that I didn't see stars like those in LA. I stared up at them until I was dizzy. Except for the Big and Little Dippers, I couldn't name a constellation. I wondered if I would ever learn to name the stars.

He told me that he knew it wasn't easy for me to leave. "You want to see them back together, anyone would," he said. "But it's not as simple . . ."

"As a movie," I said.

"I guess that's right," he said.

I looked at him standing there. His hands were at his sides, drumming his thighs. I think he was nervous in my presence after all the secrets he had tried to keep from me. And I didn't feel that I could trust him.

I started to say something, something meaningless just to relieve the tension between us. But he interrupted me. "I know you don't have a very high opinion of me," he said.

"Don't worry," I said. "I'm nobody, really."

"That's not true," He said. "I just want you to know that I *have* tried to save my brother. I would gladly change places with him if that would help. People don't understand how anyone can live the way he lives, but he's found something with those people, I think. He takes care of the younger ones. I bring him to my place as often as he'll let me and get him cleaned up, dressed in decent clothes. I always try to keep him from going back."

He stopped, and I told him that I understood.

"No," he said, "nobody can understand, really. Sometimes *I* don't understand."

The last thing we did at the cottage was take the things from the bureau in the maid's room and put them in Warren's car. Then we walked slowly through every room, reassuring ourselves that they bore no trace of his brother. When I said good-bye to him I told him that it was really none of my business what happened in this cottage. "I think I blew it all out of perspective over the years, Warren. I made it into some beautiful, romantic thing. I'm going home where I belong," I said.

He just nodded and looked into my eyes. He said that next summer he might talk to whoever was in charge of hiring my father's replacement. He wanted to know if I'd write a letter on his behalf.

"Of course," I said.

"Well then, maybe I'll call you?"

"Call me," I said.

"I really appreciate that," he said. "The caretaker's job would be a way for me to keep an eye on my brother's daughter. To see that she always has what she needs."

I told him that I understood, and I asked him if he would shut down the cottage after Christmas. "I talked to Katherine last night, and she may not come after all," I told him. "She said she might go some place warm for Christmas."

He nodded. "That might be better," he said. "Don't worry. I'll wait until after Christmas, and then I'll close the place up."

I thanked him for his help. "Take care of yourself," I said.

"You too," he told me.

I was going to add more water to the rink every few hours through the night, so I slept in my clothes, not even bothering to take off my boots.

On my second trip the moon was right overhead, lighting the spray of water from the hose. Some men are making money right now, I said to myself. I'm making ice.

In the morning I packed up my things. The bed frame I left as it was. And the sleeping bag.

It was in honor of my father's memory that I took the time to decorate the Christmas tree in the widow's walk as he and I had done together once. When I finished I stood at the windows looking back toward the city, then out over Rose Point. At the white strand of beach where waves were running up onto the shore. The golf course, carved out among thick stands of white birch and pine trees, was under fresh snow. I saw the yacht club with its gray docks pulled up onshore and tied down. The narrow bicycle paths winding through the bird sanctuary. The tall, pitched roof of the library. The open fields where the snow lay evenly. And the stately cottages standing in the winter light. I wondered if I would ever see this place again.

I walked through the cottage one more time, feeling a part of myself in the rooms, along with my father. And it was a good feeling, and it surprised me and made me think that I had changed in some way in the days since I'd returned here.

25

As soon as I got in the car and turned on the radio there was news of the storm. It was sweeping up the eastern seaboard, gale warnings had been posted for all of coastal Maine. The radio said that half a foot of snow had already fallen in Philadephia, and in Providence and Hartford snow was falling at a rate of one inch per hour.

I stopped at the yacht club and walked down the pier to the harbor. The sky was clear and pale blue overhead, without even the faintest trace of a breeze. The sea was flat, the wooden dorys of the fishermen swung gently on their mooring lines. All the way across the cove the sky was blue except for a plum-colored light at the horizon. I looked down at a brown duck leading four babies toward the shore, her head turning from side to side, watching for trouble. I thought about Olivia standing here with her mother, throwing crusts of bread into the water.

The highway south was clear all the way to Kittery, and I didn't let the car slip below eighty miles per hour. I was driving fast to try to keep myself from losing my resolve. I wanted to honor Warren's wishes, and I knew that if I didn't leave Rose Point behind me, I wouldn't be able to keep myself from telling Katherine about her father. *This time, a clean break from the past,* I kept telling myself. I had held on long enough to the world at Rose Point, a world that had never included me except in my illusions of the place and the people who lived there briefly.

When I crossed the bridge into Massachusetts the sky darkened quickly and the snow began coming down hard on a slanting wind. In the distance the lights of Boston appeared and then vanished as if they were blinking off and on. I was in a line of traffic behind a snowplow, and we were moving slower and slower.

As soon as the signs for Logan airport began appearing, the traffic coming toward me grew heavy, and I had a sense that something was wrong.

Just outside the Ted Williams Tunnel two state troopers were stopping cars.

"Airport's closed," one of them said to me.

"For how long?"

"Indefinitely. A plane skidded across the main runway."

"Can I get a flight to LA from anywhere else?"

"Providence will be shut down by the time you get there. New York's been reopened. That's your only shot."

Normally you figure Boston to New York is a four-hour drive, four and a half at the most. I knew it might take me twice as long today, which would make it six in the evening when I reached JFK airport.

I lost an hour just getting back through the tunnel. Cars were crawling along as if their drivers had never seen snow before. As soon as I reached an opening I pulled into the passing lane and pushed the accelerator down. My rear wheels slid to the left and I brought them back slowly, the way my father had taught me when I was seventeen and first learning to drive on winter roads. All I could see of the cars I was passing were the white cones of their headlights. When I finally pulled even with the snowplow, trying to pass it, the driver laid on his horn. He kept blowing it. Finally, I caught a glimpse of him. He had rolled down his window and was waving his hand at me to stay back. I fell off and took my place in the line of cars behind him.

Just outside Providence there was a roadblock of flashing white and red lights. State troopers in black capes were directing everyone off the interstate.

"Turnpike's closed, sir," one said to me.

"I have to get to New York," I told him.

"Route One. But you'll never make it past Newport," he said.

For a long time I couldn't go faster than twenty miles an hour without the back end of the car fishtailing right and left. At a 7-Eleven store I stopped for coffee. "I hope it's strong," I told him. "I've got a hard road in front of me and I'm falling asleep."

"We've got some of these no-doze pills," he said.

I bought a pack and swallowed three inside the store.

Back on the highway I was down to under twenty miles an hour. The blowing snow, the cadence of the windshield wipers, and the effect of the pills made me feel disconnected from time and more awake than the world around me.

It grew dark and I hadn't reached the border of Connecticut, impossible as this was for me to comprehend. I found myself dreaming my way through the storm, when suddenly I saw bright lights way out ahead, off in the distance, burning through the darkness and the blowing snow. I was feeling the loneliness of the road, and these lights cheered me, the thought that they might be the town of Cumberland, Rhode Island, where I once had spent time with a good friend from college. I drove faster, eager to come upon that town again. But soon the lights up ahead became too bright to be a town, and my spirits began to sink again. And then I came upon it—a concrete fortress of storage vaults standing high up on a hill, surrounded by a chain-link fence and the blinding arc lights that one associates with prisons. I pulled off to the side of the road and stared at the structure, and I could not account for why it made me feel so empty. These vaults were going up across the country now that Americans were accumulating more possessions than their houses could hold. As I sat there I thought of Charles Halworth and all the homeless, lost people like him somehow finding the keys to these storage bins where they could spend their winters. I began to feel very small, the way I had in the hospital morgue. Small and stripped of something essential. I felt like I had no breath left in my lungs, and that I would not breathe again until I took hold of something meaningful.

I began to drive harder through the white night. I kept pressing down the accelerator, but for some reason I was unable to close the distance; the miles seemed to be dividing and multiplying while I was frozen in place on a road that kept moving out ahead of me, pouring out of itself and spreading farther and farther into the distance.

Maybe I had my eyes shut for an instant, I don't know. Suddenly I swerved out of the way of a man who jumped into the road, waving his arms and running straight for me. He pounded on the roof when I slid past him, and I stopped and got out of the car as quickly as I could, swearing at him under my breath until the helpless look in his eyes made me pause.

He grabbed my left arm desperately. "Please," he said, "I need help."

He pointed to where he had left his car on the side of

the highway. We ran in that direction, but we couldn't find it. The blowing snow stung my face each time I raised my head. I was holding onto his wool topcoat just above his elbow, half expecting that he would vanish and that I had been dreaming the whole thing.

Finally, I heard him say, "There! Over there, I see it."

2 6

The whole time we were trying to push his car out of the snowbank along the guardrail, I was aware of the time passing minute by minute, and of the path that led to California blowing shut.

"Do you think we'll get it?" he asked me. He was breathing very hard.

"It's no use," I told him. "We'll take my car."

"I don't know," he said frantically. "Maybe if we keep pushing."

"Look," I said, "where are you trying to get to?"

"Ridgewood, New Jersey."

"How far past the city?"

"An hour."

"Come on, get in my car. I'll take you as far as I can."

"My books," he said with panic in his eyes. "I have books in my car. I can't leave them."

"Books?" I said. "They'll be there when you get your car back."

"You don't understand," he told me. "I can't leave them here."

I helped him take three enormous cardboard boxes from his trunk and put them into mine.

"Where are you headed?" he asked me, when we were in my car.

"The airport."

"JFK and LaGuardia are both shut down," he said. "It was on the radio."

We came up with a plan that had him getting a bus from the airport and me waiting there until I could catch a plane home. I drove blind for the next hour, the whole world reduced to snow swirling madly through the paths of my headlights, while he asked me one question after another, maybe just to reassure himself by keeping me awake. He wanted to know where I was coming from and where I was going, and once I began talking, the whole story of Charles Halworth and his daughter just poured out of me as if I'd been waiting for him to come along to tell it to.

"That's really something," he said.

"It is, I know," I said. "But I still don't understand why he's living in the streets and why he wouldn't want to see his daughter now, after all these years apart."

He shrugged, and said, "Simple. He gave up his daughter in order to protect her from himself. Makes perfect sense to me. Figure it this way: Living in the streets, you're not going to hurt anybody. You're just going to hurt yourself."

I turned and looked at him nodding his head, satisfied with his answer.

"What about you?" I said. "Tell me about yourself." And it was a relief to hear his voice replace my own.

He got into it quickly, telling me that he was a salesman, and had been for all of his working years.

"I'm a road man," he told me.

"That must be rough on your family," I said.

"Yeah. Yeah, it sure is. My wife used to tell people that I had a magic touch when it came to selling. I'd head off on a sales trip and I'd ask her how much money she wanted me to bring home this time. She'd name a figure and I'd get it for her. Right on the button. But lately I haven't been doing that well. I think my luck has run out."

"We all go through slumps," I said. "What is it you sell?"

"Books. The books in your trunk. Very expensive Torahs."

"Torahs?"

"Yes, the Jewish bible. That's why I couldn't leave them in my car back there. They're very expensive. Did you know that when a Torah is worn out, you don't throw it away, you bury it?"

He paused for a moment. "We're all salesmen aren't we?" he said.

He stopped talking for a while, and in the sudden

silence the sound of the windshield wipers seemed to grow louder and louder.

"So," I said to break the silence, "on this trip how many Torahs did you sell?"

"None," he said grimly. "I've got seventy-two in my boxes back there, same number I started out with. The trouble is, I decided I had to do something with my hair before I made my first calls. It's going all gray now. I was going to do Greenwich, Connecticut, the next day. So I bought some dye, and my first night I was in this Red Roof Motel putting the stuff in my hair, and I got it all over my hands. They make it look so easy to put in on the ads on television."

He held his hands up to the dashboard light. "It's still there," he said. "I couldn't go into people's living rooms with my hands all black, not in Greenwich."

He looked at his hands a moment longer, then put them in his coat pockets. "But tell me," he said, "don't you think you should go back to Maine?"

"What do you mean?"

"I don't know, I'm down on my luck right now and I'm not sure of too many things. But that man and his daughter need each other, don't they? And you're the person who can bring them together. There's a passage in the Torah that I was reading the other night. It asks us to think about how differently we would live a single day in our lives if we knew it was our last day."

At the airport he decided to rent a car instead of waiting for a bus. When we were finished loading his books into the trunk, he put his hand on my shoulder and thanked me for taking him this far. He handed me his business card. "Have a safe trip," he said. "And write to me sometime so I know how things turned out."

I went so far as to drive my car onto the rental lot to return it. I opened the door and looked at the airport terminal, snow piled high on its flat roof. There was a buzzing in my head, and for some reason I began to divide the airport roof into sections, trying to calculate how long it would take me to shovel all the snow off. I thought about what Callie Boardman had said to me, how she hoped that I could stop running away. Then I thought about sitting in the airport terminal all night while Katherine was just a short drive from here. I had her address in Manhattan. I wanted to see her face before I left. So I got back in the car and headed for the city.

2 7

It was three in the morning when I got to the apartment. A man wearing a black cape with gold epaulets swung open the door for me.

"I'm sure they're sleeping now," he said, when I told him who I had come to see.

"I'll see them in the morning," I said. "Would it be all right if I sleep in the lobby here?"

He got me a blanket and I laid down on a couch beside a Christmas tree.

As soon as I awoke I knew that I had slept much too long.

There was a woman on duty now. "Gone," she said when I told her who I had come to see. "They left about two hours ago."

"*Gone?*" I said.

"Where did you come from?" she asked.

"Maine," I said.

"Maine? That's where they went. In this storm, can you believe that? I tried to tell them—"

I cut her off before she could finish. "What kind of car?"

"Car? No. A limousine."

I began driving north then, back to Maine. It was just past seven o'clock. Slush on the highway had frozen, and every so often the rear wheels of the car would lift off the road and float momentarily until I raised my foot off the accelerator. The daylight improved visibility only slightly, so that from the passing lane I caught a glimpse of each car just before it vanished again. By now there were very few cars on the highway, and each time one came into view ahead of me, I pushed the gas pedal harder until I caught up with it. When I was sure it was not a limousine I pulled away and watched it disappear in the rearview mirror.

I don't know why I thought I even had a chance to catch up to them; years of chasing after whatever I wanted and getting it, I suppose. I ended up losing all the time that I had gained when, somewhere outside Worcester, Massachusetts, the car I caught up with there turned out to be a state police cruiser.

"You got something against Christmas?" the officer asked when I rolled down my window.

A wise guy, I thought. I turned and stared out at the snow until I felt dizzy. I had to fight the desire to argue with him. When he asked me again if I had something against Christmas, I said, "No sir."

"The way you're driving, you won't live to see it."

"It's a long story," I said. "I need to get to Maine."

"License," he said.

I handed it to him through the open window. I watched snow land on it as he stood there looking at my name.

"Terry McQuinn," he said. "Running back. Brown University. Nineteen seventy-three through nineteen seventy-seven."

I was astonished. "You must be the only person in New England to follow Brown football."

"My nephew was on that team. Eric Guckain."

"Tackle on the right side," I said.

"That's the guy. People said you were the best that ever played there. Should have made the All-American team but you mouthed off to too many referees."

"Some of that might be true."

"Big chip on your shoulder."

He took his time walking around the car to the passenger's side. He got in slowly. When he sat down his dark blue pants rode up his legs.

"Is this a rental car?" he asked me.

"I'm trying to catch up to a woman in a limousine," I said.

"Aren't we all?" he said. "I hope she's worth a hundred-and-forty-dollar ticket."

I told him the whole story. I saw sorrow sweep across his face like a dark shadow. "What year was the accident?" he asked me.

"Nineteen sixty-three."

"Spell the guy's last name for me."

I told him.

"Let's get in my cruiser," he said.

A box of Kentucky Fried Chicken was on the seat between us. He got on his radio.

"*H* as in happy, *A* as in apple, *L* as in Lincoln, *W* as in witness, O-R-T-H," he said. "I'll wait."

He told me it would take a few minutes. "So," he said, "this daughter's got the big house in Maine now?"

"Yeah, that's right."

"So, she's rich?"

"I suppose."

"What's she think of you?"

"I don't know. If you let me catch her, I'll try and find out."

He laughed. Then a voice came on the radio. "Halworth, Charles, 004-50-6675. Leaving the scene of an accident. December 24, 1963. Portland, Maine."

"Bingo," he said.

I thought of Warren telling me what my father had said to him, how no one should ever be completely forgotten.

The radio voice came on again. "Damn. It's getting worse. Attempted kidnapping. New York City. June 1967," he repeated for me. "All charges dropped, August same year. Does this sound like your man?"

I was lost for a while, wondering how he had gone about trying to take his daughter from her mother.

"So, when you catch up to this gal, what are you going to do?" he asked.

It took me a second to realize where I was and who was talking to me. *"Do?"* I said. "I don't know. I guess I'm going to make sure she's okay after all these years, then head back home."

He nodded his head and adjusted his hat again. "Look," he said, "why don't you follow me and we'll see if we can catch her?"

He ripped the speeding ticket in half. "You got any kids who play football?"

"No," I said.

"Shame. I'll take you as far as the border," he said, giving me his hand to shake.

He turned on his flashing red and white lights. I followed him for eighty miles, driving very fast through the snow while he led the way.

2 8

As I saw the gate to Rose Point up ahead of me, I felt like I was coming out of a fever dream, stunned by the miles and hours without sleep, the numbing effect of driving blind, staring into swirling snow. For the last six hours I had driven hard, bearing down on the peaceful stillness of Rose Point and the presence of a woman who was a little girl when I last saw her.

It was two in the afternoon. The storm had blown off shore and a hard winter light, amber in shade, had seeped through the clouds. I was climbing over the gate to walk to my father's shop for the key when I heard a sound enter this silent world, the sound of a dog barking.

From behind the snow-covered pine trees on a small promontory overlooking the harbor, I saw a black limousine parked at the shore alongside the granite rocks that protected the east side of the harbor. There was a white rowboat tied to its roof.

Just beyond the limousine I saw a woman and a child. "It's them," I said, out loud. In an instant I felt the exhaustion leave me, replaced by such a surge of hope that I had to concentrate to catch my breath.

Katherine was holding the hand of her small child in red puddle boots that matched her own. She wore a long denim dress and a navy blue coat that fell below her waist. Her dark hair was in a braid. How could I help but wonder at once about her husband, imagining that he was in an office somewhere thinking about her and about the child. Maybe he would arrive by the weekend, in time to spend Christmas beside these people he belonged with. Perhaps he and I would shake hands. He would thank me for the work I had done.

These thoughts knocked something down inside me. What right had I to be here except my father's right, the right of the caretaker?

There was a yellow dog running around them in wild, ecstatic loops, dipping its nose in the waves, biting at the snow, then charging back to lick the child's face and bark encouragement. I remembered what Katherine had told me when we spoke last. How she believed her days at the point would be live-over days for Olivia and for her. I hadn't really known what she had meant until I saw them on the shore where, it seemed, some aspect of them was being completed even as I watched. I would have gladly opened the *Serenity* cottage a hundred times for this chance to be here spying on their pleasure.

Katherine looked happy, as you would expect. But I

saw her weariness as well. She sat down on the rocks, not bothering to clear away the snow. She took the child into her arms and stared out at Pumpkin Island, which lay a half mile off shore. She rocked her daughter slowly in her arms. She lay her cheek against the top of the child's head.

Then the driver came out of the limousine, a tall barrel-chested man, as big as an opera tenor, dressed in black and wearing a chauffeur's cap. He began untying the ropes that held the skiff on the roof. It seemed odd to me that anyone living in New York City would have a boat, and even if they did, why would they bring it to Maine in the winter? I saw Katherine glance at him, then turn back to look toward the island again as if she were waiting for someone to appear there.

The yellow retriever ran to the driver's side, watching curiously as he slid the boat off the roof, onto the ground. The driver took oars from the trunk of the limousine and then stood quietly a moment with his hands clasped behind his back. Like a soldier, I thought, someone hired not simply to drive Katherine and her daughter from here to there but to protect them.

Some time passed before she stood up. Carefully she took the child by both hands and led her to the skiff one step at a time. She pushed her gently toward the middle seat several times, and when the child didn't move, she lifted her by her arms and placed her in the boat. She kept one hand on the child's arm as she stepped into the boat herself. She took hold of the oars and placed the child's hands beside her own and together they pretended to row. After a moment she waved to the driver, and then the child waved too, as if they were leaving him behind and heading out to sea in the boat.

The driver called to them, and this made the child wave even harder. I had a sense that there was something wrong with Olivia, though I couldn't have known for sure. It was the way her mother and the driver tried so hard to persuade her to join them in their excitement.

The driver lingered a few moments before Katherine gestured for him to drive on. He returned to the car and drove away, slowly.

When it was just the two of them I saw more clearly that there was something remarkable in the way they moved through the light, some inexplicable pattern to their movements, like they were bound awkwardly to one another, with none of the grace one expects to find between a mother and her child. As if the child were falling and the mother were trying to catch her before she struck the ground. It took me by surprise. Though I had spent no time with little children, Olivia entered my consciousness the way a far-off sound—a train whistle in the dead of night—will reach you at such a deep level it seems to be calling just to you.

As the driver passed from their view, rounding the far

corner of the lane, Olivia placed her hands against her eyes. Katherine reacted at once, moving them away from her face. She leaned forward and said something to her before she stepped out of the boat. Then she took the child's hands and helped her out.

I expected Olivia to run down the beach to the breaking waves. But she walked slowly, just a step behind her mother, with her arms out in front of her.

Like watching darkness fall, I observed all of this. I kept my place there on the hill, waiting for something that I couldn't name. And feeling inadequate, incapable of knowing what I should have known.

They knelt in the sand for a little while, and then Katherine lifted her daughter into her arms and carried her back up the shore.

Turning my back to the sea, I watched them coming up the rocks before they disappeared down Winslow Homer Lane. Two people who didn't know me and who could not have understood why I turned my car around and drove away.

The city streets were piled high with snow. Along the sidewalks a narrow path had been cleared for shoppers and office workers walking with their heads down against a stiff wind that shook the street signs and traffic lights. I passed up several hotels that looked forlorn and deserted in the winter light, until I came to one that seemed right. The Regency was a broad and handsome brick building with arched doors and a circular drive in front made of polished black marble and lit by old-fashioned gas lamps. At the desk a young woman, college age, asked me if I wanted a room that looked into the square.

"The square?" I said.

"The Christmas tree in Monument Square," she said, smiling at me.

"Yes," I told her eagerly.

I paid for six nights, through Christmas, and asked her if the front door was locked after a certain hour.

"Midnight," she said. "But your key opens it."

"I'm going to need two keys," I said, and I told her that I would be meeting another person during my stay.

"I can give you an extra key for your friend, or you can leave his name here at the desk," she said. "We'll call you in your room and get permission to send him up."

I explained that I wanted my friend to be able to come and go as he pleased. "Just so long as he can use the room when I'm out, whatever would be easier," I said.

"I should write his name here then," she said, taking a journal with a leather cover from beneath the counter.

"Charles Halworth," I told her. As she wrote his name I told her that I wanted him to be able to charge incidentals to my room account. For this I had to sign a special invoice.

I had no idea, really, what I was doing, and until the elevator doors closed and I began to rise from the lobby, I expected to be stopped and questioned further by a manager.

The room was very nice. Two large queen-size beds, a mahogany desk and bureau, three modest oil paintings of a beach, a boathouse, and a pile of driftwood. A wall of windows reflected the colored lights of the tree in Monument Square, as promised.

I stood at the windows for quite some time. As I watched, a city employee in a dark green quilted jacket with a fur-lined collar climbed up the statue of Longfellow and placed three beautifully wrapped Christmas packages on his lap.

At a swanky men's store an irrepressible little man no more than five feet tall spent an hour with me. I guessed at Charles Halworth's size, figuring him to be just slightly larger than me. We began with seven pairs of dark, ribbed wool socks and seven pairs of plaid boxer shorts, then worked our way to pleated and cuffed corduroy trousers in olive green, black, and tan colors. Navy blue and wheat cable-knit sweaters. Half a dozen cotton oxford shirts, a Harris tweed sport coat, and a dark blue cashmere topcoat that looked like Mr. Halworth's ragged one might have looked when it was new. We had approximated the size of a man slightly larger than me, and when we were finished we laid everything out across a table stacked with brightly colored sweaters that the manager said were ladder-stitched. "What do you think?" he asked me, sweeping his hand over our selection.

"What do I think?" I said. "I think I'm crazy."

"Pardon me, sir?"

"Nothing. Nothing. Now suits," I said. And these took some time. He tried hard to reassure me with words like, "classic" and "conventional," but nothing seemed right.

"Very well," He said, undefeated. "We don't know the gentleman's profession, but perhaps we know the occasion? Office party? Dinner party? Travel?"

"Reunion," I told him.

I had a simple plan for later tonight. I would find Charles Halworth in the parking garage. I would tell him that I was a rich man who wanted to do something good at

Christmas. How could he say no to this? I would install him in room 603 at the Regency, where he would dress in his new clothes and wait for me to come by and take him to Rose Point, thus delivering him into the world of the blessed, into the arms of his daughter and granddaughter. And we would all spend Christmas together at the cottage.

It was, at best, a childishly simple plan. I knew it would never work, and yet I could not resist it.

In the hotel room I ordered dinner and a bottle of wine and ate sitting at the window. The time and temperature blinked from the roof of a tall building across the square: 7:14 P.M. -13°F. It could just as easily have been seven in the morning. I wondered what time Katherine would put her daughter to bed, and which bedrooms she would choose. The cottage would be unbearably cold unless they had all five fireplaces going. Two of the bedrooms had electric heat, something I should have told her. And the pipes . . . I worried about the pipes as I tried on one of the sweaters and stood in front of the mirror. A nice sweater, I thought. The kind that the summer people at Rose Point wore.

I lay down on one of the beds and closed my eyes to take an hour nap. Just before I fell asleep I thought about what it would be like to give up and live in the streets. To lose my will to work, and to never earn another penny. What if I were to stay in this small city, spending every penny of my savings and investments, and then the cash advances from my credit cards. How long would my money last at $185 a night plus meals? Say, $225 a day. Say, I could come up with $450,000 dollars. How long would it last?

When I did the math I was amazed to find that it broke down exactly to two thousand days. Just over five years, which would make me forty-three years old. Then I figured Mr. Halworth's age. He was a young father when I met him in 1963. Twenty-seven. Twenty-eight. By now, late fifties. I would have youth on my side, but still, what would it be like to willingly descend the levels of comfort and respectability, and to finally spend the last night in this room, knowing that in the morning I would begin living in the streets?

When I awoke it was three in the morning. I swore at myself and drove around the city from one parking garage to the another. They were all locked and the streets were empty.

Soon I was in my father's shop starting a fire in the wood-stove. I assured myself that the next night I would try again. I stared into the flames and thought of the room at the hotel, and of the new clothes hanging there. If you had said to me that I was still trying to turn Charles Halworth's life into a movie, that I had prepared the set and his costume, and that I was waiting for him to act out the part of a good father, I would have said you were wrong. Watching Katherine on the shore had convinced me that she needed her father.

3 0

I stood outside the cottage the next morning watching her walk toward me, holding her daughter's hand. I studied Katherine's black hair, the way a few loose strands had curled in the moist air. And her long fingers. And the way the cold had colored her cheeks red.

I heard the hard-packed snow creak like wooden stairs beneath her feet. "I'm Katherine," she said, offering me her hand. She seemed pleased to see me. "I thought we were alone here," she said. "Have you come to Maine for Christmas?"

It took me a moment to realize that she thought I was another resident. "I'm Terry McQuinn," I said, taking off my father's glove and holding out my hand for her to shake.

She looked surprised. "You didn't go back to California?"

"The storm," I said. "The airports were closed."

"Brought together by a storm?" she said, as if she were thinking out loud.

"Fate," I said.

"Do you believe in it?"

"Of course."

"Well, this is my good fortune," she said, smiling. "I've put you to so much trouble though."

"No," I said. "It's been good work."

Just then I remembered the last time we spoke. "I'm sorry about that last call. I'm not a drinker, really."

"Don't be sorry," she said.

She looked into my eyes, holding me in her gaze. Then she turned and looked back at the cottage above us, gently tipping the child's head so that her eyes were on the house.

"Isn't it something," Katherine exclaimed. "What is it, Olivia?" she asked the child.

"My castle," the child said, with delight. "C for castle."

"C for castle, that's right, Teapot," Katherine said.

I watched Olivia press her fists up against her eyes. Katherine responded immediately by gently pulling them away. "What else lives in the C book?" she asked.

"Cake. Cake and cars!" Olivia said proudly.

"Yes! Yes," her mother said. Then, in quick succession the child's fists flew against her eyes again, and Katherine moved them, holding them back the last time.

"And curtains," Olivia said. "And Carmel, California."

Katherine took her in her arms. "Oh yes," she said. It

was as if I had vanished and it was only the two of them. She was smiling when she kissed Olivia's cheek, but when she turned and looked at me, I saw the smile fading.

I was reluctant to say anything.

"Did you freeze last night?" I asked.

"We were fine," she said. "Olivia and I slept in the blue bed. Didn't we love your grandmother's old blue bed?"

"Cambridge, England," Olivia said.

"It's the *Encyclopedia Britannica*," Katherine said to me. "We made poor Lawrence bring the whole set to Maine with us."

Lawrence. I took a chance and asked. "Is Lawrence your husband?"

"Oh," she replied. "Poor, dear Lawrence. I don't think he would wish to be my husband in a thousand years. I drive him crazy as it is. He helps us get around."

"He drove you, that's right," I said hopefully.

"It's just the three of us," she went on. "He's in town getting warm. Lawrence has a tolerance for many things. Tobacco. Alcohol. Poker. But not for the cold. He was shivering like a schoolboy, so I ordered him to town."

She seemed a brave and stoic traveler. She had those sea-green eyes you seldom encounter. So green you had to look again to be sure. And each time she smiled, it surprised me that I wished my father were here to see her. I pictured him carrying the Christmas tree lights and the angel up to the widow's walk in preparation for her visit.

Placing Charles Halworth's things in the white bureau for her to discover. Setting up the stage as I had done at the hotel for her father.

"Come closer," she said to me suddenly. "Come meet Olivia."

I didn't know how close to come. I took a step, and then another when she gestured with her hand. "Come close," she said again.

When she was satisfied, she nodded.

"Olivia," I said. "It's a lovely name."

Katherine thanked me. "You see, Mommy gave you a lovely name," she said to her daughter. "This is Mr. McQuinn," she said. But the child would not look at me.

I asked her to please call me by my first name. "Whenever you say 'Mr. McQuinn,' I think my father must be standing behind me." There must have been an edge to those words because she turned at once and faced me with a curious expression.

"I'm sorry, Terry," she said. Then she touched Olivia's face. "Terry opened your grandmother's castle for us."

"I loved your message," I said to Olivia. "And I left you a beep. Several beeps, in fact. Did you hear my beeps?"

She nodded her head. Then Katherine took her hands from her eyes again. "Feel Mr. McQuinn's hands, Olivia," she said.

I held them up and the little girl touched them the way you might touch delicate china.

"You can know a man by his hands," Katherine said. "Mr. McQuinn is a caretaker, Olivia. Feel these marvelous hands." Katherine ran her fingers over the stitches on my thumb. "Was that our fault?" she asked.

"My fault," I said. "I wasn't paying attention. I'm not a real caretaker, I'm afraid."

She moved her daughter's fists from her eyes again and said, "In our book you are."

"I want my book, Mommy," Olivia said. "I want my C book."

"Tonight, sweetheart. Not now. We have so much exploring to do."

She smiled and said she had been walking from room to room in the cottage, looking for signs that she had been there as a child. This took my breath away.

"My mother swears I never was," she said. "But she revises history. Still, I didn't find anything broken."

I asked her what she meant by this. Before she answered she set Olivia down and took the child's cane from inside her coat. Without saying a word, she placed it in Olivia's hands and the child wandered off.

"I was the terror of the neighborhood when I was a kid," she said to me. "I broke everything. There's always one like that in every neighborhood, I've learned. I'd borrow a friend's bicycle and the tire would go flat. Parents used to groan when I showed up. Doorknobs fell off in my hands. Lamps tipped over. I couldn't help it; it wasn't my fault. I just moved too fast, I guess. At the Mahoney house I was only allowed in the basement."

She was laughing now. And smiling. I watched her and thought of the resilience of her spirit.

"If you found anything broken when you were opening the cottage, I must have been here."

"But you weren't ever here before?"

"No. Apparently not."

"And your mother just told you about the place?"

"Last month, before she and her new husband left for England. I think she felt sorry for us."

She said nothing for a moment, and I watched with her as Olivia walked a little ways away from us. She walked slowly in the deep snow. When she seemed to going straight for a birch tree, I began to say something. Katherine raised her hand for me to wait. "No," she whispered. "She'll find her way."

And she did. The tip of her cane struck the tree, then Olivia reached out and touched it. She stood there for several minutes running her hands over the bark.

"Does she see anything?" I asked.

"Not any more," she said. "Until she was a year old she could see bright lights. I was teaching her colors. But we didn't finish."

I told her I was sorry and she looked at me, this time as if she had just remembered that I was standing next to her.

"She's the reason I finally got to see Maine," she said

happily. "I've always wanted to come to Maine, and we brought a skiff with us."

"A skiff?" I said, stupidly.

"A rowboat. You're not a sailor?"

"No, I'm afraid I never spent any time around boats. But where did you find a boat in New York City?"

"It was at my mother's place, outside the city. Tell me though, Terry, you grew up here and no one ever took you sailing?"

"It wasn't even close," I told her. "I lived in a different world."

"What a shame," she said earnestly. "My mother deserves a firing squad at sunrise for her many—for a life of atrocious behavior—but her one virtue is that she taught me to sail."

She paused momentarily, then continued to tell me that she had to row out to Pumpkin Island. "The first thing we did when we got here yesterday was walk on the beach and look out at the island. My mother claims to have buried her pet dog on Pumpkin Island when she was a little girl. You see, when she told me about this house I thought for certain she was making the whole thing up. Then she told me about the dog's grave, and I assured her that I would check to see if her story held any water. You'll have to come with us. I found life jackets in the carriage house. One small enough to fit Olivia, which must have been for my mother when she was a child."

"How long has the cottage been in her family?" I asked.

"My understanding is that my mother's grandfather bought it after making a fortune inventing the little tire patching kits that became a standard item in every Ford that rolled off the assembly line."

"Amazing," I said, and I did find this amazing.

"Yes," she said. "At least he didn't manufacture something reprehensible. I *am* thankful for that."

By now Olivia had found her way across the snow-covered lawn to the skating rink. We watched her kneel down and touch the ice with both hands. Then she leaned over and pressed her face to it.

"I should get us ready," Katherine said. "Would you like to travel with us to Pumpkin Island?"

I wondered briefly how many ways I could embarrass myself in a boat. "I wouldn't miss it," I said. "It might be a live-over journey, especially with me aboard."

She was so pleased with this. "Our *live-over* days in Maine. You remembered," she said, without taking her eyes off her daughter. Then she spoke again as if I weren't there. "I took my daughter to the best facility in the world for blind children. When we first arrived the director spoke to all of us in an auditorium. Olivia and I were in the front row. He told the children that they were going to have to learn to be twice as smart as sighted children. Twice as hardworking. Twice as strong. I was sitting there listening to this man, one of the world's great authorities on blindness, when it dawned on me that what he was saying was that my daughter was only half a person. Half a person, and so she would have to try twice as hard. It broke my heart, Terry. I took Olivia's hand and we walked out of the auditorium."

I saw her fierce determination. It seemed to deepen the green in her eyes.

"I'm not sure I did the right thing," she said, sadly. She turned then and began walking away without saying another word. As the space between us widened, I wanted to call her back and tell her that she *had* done the right thing, that feeling like half a person was exactly how I had felt about myself in comparison to the summer people at Rose Point, just as I had told Callie. Even then, in the first glimpse of the instinct she carried in her heart, I didn't want her to walk away. I watched her kneel down on the ice rink and put her arm around her daughter. I was certain the way we are about some things, sure that the sight of them would be enough to draw Charles Halworth back to the world of the hopeful and the loved. And so long as they were here, in the cottage, just down the lane from me, they were not lost to him. They would never be lost to him as long as I knew where they were.

I met the limousine coming the other way on the lane as I walked back to my father's shop. I waved, the car rolled to a stop, and the driver's window went down, revealing Lawrence behind the wheel. He was in his fifties, a large, boxy man with silver hair slicked straight back on his head. He had a shoe box beside him on the seat. "Would you have some place to hide this until Christmas?" he asked me. He lifted the lid off the box and showed me a tiny brown rabbit, of all things, with a twitching pink nose and black eyes. "They said the only thing it needs to live a long, prosperous life is to be touched every day."

I saw the yellow dog, his face pressed to the glass panel that separated the driver from the living room behind him.

"That's Jack," Lawrence said. "He wants the bunny for lunch. Right Jack?"

He introduced himself to me as he followed me into the shop. "Lawrence Wilson at your service," he said, tipping his beret.

"You're Katherine's driver?" I said, pushing open the door.

"Newly appointed, yes," he said. "I was eighteen years with the queen mother until she shipped off for England with number six."

"Number six?"

"Husband number six," he said.

There was more than the rabbit to hide. He had been shopping at L.L. Bean and had dozens of boxes and bags in the limo's trunk. "I was too cold to sleep," he said, "and when I remembered that L.L. Bean was open twenty-four hours a day I spent the night shopping."

The gifts were for Olivia, he told me. "She has stolen my heart," he said. "But I couldn't find the one thing I was searching for."

"What was that?" I asked.

"A sled. A real sled, not a plastic one. Are you too young to remember the Flexible Flyer?"

"No, I remember them," I said. "The queen mother? Is that Mrs. Halworth?"

"No, sir. Halworth is a name she discarded five husbands ago. She's been a Tilly, a Frederick, and a Constantine since I went to work for her. Before I arrived on the scene, a Wentworth. Poor man fell off a horse in the middle of the annual country club fox hunt. I believe the fox then bit him in the hind quarters." He laughed.

"And her daughter?"

"She's got Tilly's name," he said. "That would be the husband after Halworth."

"I remember her mother when she was Halworth," I said, waiting for him to question me.

"From where?" he asked.

"Here. Thirty years ago she and her husband spent some time here." I took a certain measure of satisfaction in predating his knowledge of her.

"Thirty years ago?" he said. "You were a boy."

"My father was caretaker here. I helped him open their cottage one Christmas."

By the way he was looking at me I knew he had figured out what I was going to say next.

"Katherine would have been four or five? Did they bring her with them?" he asked.

"Yes," I said. "Why did her mother tell her she'd never been here before?" I asked him. "Do you know why she would lie about that?"

He took off his hat and sat down beside the band saw. "The father, I suppose," he said. "I'd been working for the queen about a year when I asked her about Katherine's father. None of my business, you know, but I was curious. She told me the guy was a kook, a real bad character. Trouble, you know what I mean. He'd tried to kidnap the girl once, I guess. Her mother and her second husband were on a golf course, riding in a cart with Katherine between them. The crazy man stalked them on a golf course. Wouldn't you have to be one of the world's great idiots to try and kidnap someone on a golf course?"

"Or very desperate," I said.

"I suppose. After something like that happens, what are you supposed to do?"

"Pretend he never existed?" I said.

He looked at me a moment. "I take it you disagree?"

"I don't have an opinion, Lawrence," I told him. "I'm just the caretaker."

"How do you like the work?" he asked. "And how do you ever keep warm?"

I explained that this wasn't my work.

"So," he said, "you've come back home then."

"In a way."

"And how's it feel?"

"A little strange," I said, and while he was nodding his head and looking away from me I asked him about Katherine's husband.

He raised his eyebrows. "Ah," he said. "You're interested in this, I can tell."

"Curious," I said.

"Curious. Yes. There's no husband onboard her boat, my friend. No room for one."

"Her boat? I don't understand."

"Figure of speech. She and Olivia are on a very small boat. Room for no one else."

For a while we worked together, trying to build a cage for the rabbit. I kept making mistakes and pretending they weren't mistakes, trying to save face. Finally, I confessed that I had none of my father's skills, and we used his tool chest for a cage, laying a screen window over the top and filling the bottom with wood shavings.

"That's a creature who'll be loved, right there," Lawrence said, as we finished. "You'll have to pry this bunny out of Olivia's hands. The little pirate. Be careful, she'll steal your heart."

I liked his smile and his enthusiasm. I thought that when the time came I would tell him the true story about Charles Halworth and he would understand.

"You're going to have to tell me why there's no husband," I said to him.

"The tiny boat," he said. "Remember?"

"*Was* there a husband?"

"There was an Oliver something the fourth. Engaged to be married, I take it. But when Katherine wouldn't give up the child, he took off."

"Give up the child?"

"Katherine brought her home from work, as I understand. She's a social worker, and there was this blind baby that no one wanted. Katherine took her, you know, just until they could find a foster home. You know how these things can work."

I told him that I didn't know. "So what happened?"

"She kept her. Adopted the little pirate. Oliver wasn't a bad fellow, from what I've heard. But he didn't feature raising a blind child that wasn't even his. None of us can know what we would do in a situation like that. He left. And she bought a set of encyclopedias." He paused and smiled to himself. "She's determined to teach the child as much as she can. They're up to the letter C. I brought the books along with us."

"She told me," I said to him.

"They don't sleep at night, you know. They study. All the way up it was the same thing. Chandelier. China. Chile. I got an education while I drove."

Just before he left the shop phone rang. It was one of the summer people, checking in to see how much snow had fallen on his roof in the storm. I told him that my father had died.

"I'm sorry to hear that," he said. "Will you be taking over for him?"

Before I could answer he asked me if I would be shoveling the snow off his roof today or tomorrow. "Your father always cleared my roof first," he said. "Above the billiards room there's been a problem with leakage."

"Leakage," I said, and I hung up.

"You'll hear from every one of them now," Lawrence told me. "I predict by dinner you'll hear from them all. They'll call to express their sympathy for your father, but really to make sure someone's onboard to do his work. I know rich people," he said.

Before he left he asked me if I'd told Katherine that

her mother was lying about her never being here as a child.

"I didn't," I said.

"Maybe you shouldn't," he said. "The queen mother's infamous fibbing is a sore spot for Katherine. I'd like to see her get away from all that and just be happy while we're here."

"I don't know if that's going to happen," I told him. "She told me she's going out to the island to see if her mother was lying about her childhood dog being buried there."

"Ah, shame," he said. "On it goes."

Lawrence was right about the summer people. I spent the afternoon fielding calls from them, asking me about the storm and if I was going to clear their roof. I told them I was making a list of names and that I would do my best to get to them. Each person who called wanted to know where they were on my list.

I didn't see Katherine and Olivia again that day. I shoveled snow from the Eldredge roof where the drifts reached up to my waist. From there I could see most of the cottages and more snow than I could have shoveled if I'd had the rest of the winter to finish.

3 2

"They're sleeping," Lawrence told me when I went to the cottage the next morning to borrow a teakettle. He looked at his watch. "Is it really the twenty-second?" he asked.

"It is," I told him.

"I've lost track of the days since I left the city. They'll be asleep for at least another two hours. They were up studying most of the night. So you're a tea man, are you?"

I was distracted by the thought of the two of them in the cottage, asleep somewhere above me.

"A tea man?" he said again.

"I'm sorry. Tea? No."

I told him I needed the kettle for an idea I had to make a sled for Olivia. He was curious. "You lost me somewhere between tea and sled."

"Come with me and I'll show you," I said.

"I haven't read the *Times* yet," he said. "But so what? I'm in Maine, right?"

We walked back to the shop together.

I built a simple wooden box long enough to hold some oak strips that my father had in his pile of trim boards, then propped it up above the teakettle on the woodstove as the water boiled and steam filled the box. We repeated this with six pots of water until the steam had softened the oak slats enough so we could round the ends into the shape of runners for the sled.

"How will we get them to dry in that shape?" he asked me.

"I saw my old man do this once for a curved porch railing," I told him. I drew the shape I wanted on the workbench and put in a half dozen nails at staggered intervals, then forced the strips between the nails.

"Hey," he said with surprise. "That's going to work, I believe."

"My reputation is on the line here, Lawrence," I said.

"But this is not your line of work. What do you do?"

I told him I worked in California. "I represent people in the film industry," I said, intending to be vague and hoping to leave it at that.

He was delighted. "The movies, you mean? You represent actors and actresses?"

"That's it," I said. "Producers, directors. Writers."

"Oh, I always wanted to act," he said, wistfully. "Favorite movie of all time?"

"Mine?"

"Yes."

"I don't know. I'd have to think about it."

"*Dr. Zhivago,*" he said. "*The Commitments* in second

place. I saw *Zhivago* for the first time when I was seventeen. It was in an old theater in Poughkeepsie, New York. I still think of it as where I learned the meaning of romantic love. Remember Zhivago writing poems for Laura in that house that looked like an ice castle? Divine stuff. Purely divine."

The whole time he was talking, revealing his generous heart to me, I wanted to tell him what I knew about Katherine's father. Maybe I should have. And maybe I should have told him what I had felt when I first saw her and her daughter on the shore. I didn't say anything because I wasn't sure how he would react. But what I wanted to tell him was that standing in front of the cottage with Katherine and Olivia had made me feel that I would remember them always, as long as I lived, and if it took until the end of my life to reconcile Katherine and her father to their past, I would patiently try.

I called my office that afternoon. There were forty-three messages on my voice mail. It took some time to go through them all, and in the end there was only one that I cared enough about to return, an actor I had been through good times and bad times with, mostly bad times for the past five years. "I screwed the audition," he said to me when I called him back. "And I *had* it, Terry, I swear, they wanted to *give* me the bloody part."

"They'll be other parts, Lewis."

"No, Terry. I'm going to kill myself tonight."

"Not tonight," I told him. "There's something big coming your way. I can feel it. Have faith."

"In what?" he asked.

"Yourself."

"I can't," he told me, softly.

I could feel the anguish in his voice. "Okay then, Lewis, have faith in me. I'll make some calls."

"No. You're going to have to dump me, Terry. I haven't earned you a dime in years."

"I'm with you until the end, Lewis. For the duration. So hang in there."

I wrote his name on my father's workbench and told myself to call him in a day or two. The truth is, there wasn't a casting person in town I could lean on to get him work. He was fifty now, at the dark turn in the road.

I caught myself talking to the rabbit about Lewis while I sanded the seat for Olivia's sled. "Let's see, Mr. Rabbit, who still owes me a favor in the city of angels?"

Before I could come up with a single name, there was a knock at the door, and there she was. A streak of red sky behind her. She said she only had a moment and she was smiling at me in a way that made me feel she was pleased to see me.

"I went by the cottage earlier," I said. "Did you sleep well?"

"Like bears," she said. "The air is so wonderful here."

I asked her to sit, but she didn't. And then I wondered
if she had smiled at me a moment earlier because she was
glad to see me or if I had read too much into this.

She wanted to know if I had any interest in going into
the city with them tonight. "Do you know Dylan
Thomas's, 'A Child's Christmas in Wales?'"

Maybe I should have told her the truth, that I'd repre-
sented the director who did the adaptation for network
television.

"I know the story, yes," was all I said.

"I've always wanted Olivia to see it," she said, "and it's
playing in the city tonight."

We stood together on the stairs of the shop before she
left. She gestured beyond the harbor toward the River
Road, where there was a small development of ranch
houses. "I guess those would be the real folks out beyond
the castle walls," she said.

I named the families for her. The Sullivans, whose
daughter Mary Lou had once won the Miss Maine con-
test. Paul Joseph, who built race cars out of junkers.
Link and Julie Cutler, who lived in the church one winter
when their trailer burned to the ground. I had gone to
school with the kids who grew up in those houses. To
them the summer people at Rose Point had the allure of
royalty.

"I ran away from those people," I told her. She turned
and looked at me.

"To find fame and fortune?"

"I don't know anymore. I think I used to know, but maybe I didn't."

"And what did you find?"

"No fame," I said. "A little fortune."

"In Hollywood," she said. "Lawrence told me."

"Yes," I said.

She gazed past me. "I don't think a movie could do justice to this beautiful place, do you?"

I thought a moment. "I'm glad it's real," I said.

She smiled at this and our eyes met. "Yes, me too," she said. "I didn't know what to expect, but now that I've seen Rose Point I'm making a pledge to forgive my mother all her future transgressions."

I laughed with her and told her that I still knew the names of the families in the houses across the harbor. "But I couldn't tell you who the people are in my apartment building in LA. Everyone comes and goes. There's something to be said about these people who are happy leading a simple life."

"Terry," she replied, shaking her head, "do you really believe there's any such thing as a simple life?"

She looked away before I could answer. We were silent for a while. The wind shifted and carried the scent of burning wood down the lane to where we stood.

"You got your fireplaces going?" I said.

"All five of them. I was once a Girl Scout."

"A Girl Scout. You look like a Girl Scout."

"An old one, maybe. Circles under my eyes."

"No," I said, "your eyes are beautiful." She seemed startled by what I had said. She brushed her hair back while I looked at her and thought how sad it was that her daughter would never see her eyes.

"Thank you," she said. She turned away quickly. As she went down the steps she said that she had to go get Olivia dressed. "We'll come for you at seven thirty?"

"Do I need my tux?"

She smiled. "Yes, absolutely. She lingered a moment, then she waved. "Good bye," she said.

33

Jack, the dog, sat in front with Lawrence and Olivia, with an expression on his face that said, *I could drive this thing if they'd give me a chance.* Olivia was giggling at something Lawrence said.

"I always wonder what she would think if she knew what splendor we traveled in," Katherine said.

"L," I said. "You'll get to limousine in your encyclopedias."

She looked at me knowingly. "Lawrence told you," she said. "I'm doing the best I can."

"She's a beautiful girl," I said. "And she has you."

"She is beautiful. I'm cheating though. Lately I've been skipping pages. Sometimes she catches me."

Lawrence turned up the radio. A song by the Beatles was playing. He turned it down and slid open the glass panel. "Know what the best thing in my life has been? The Beatles. Positively the best thing of all. Can you imagine, in another fifteen years, when all of us baby boomers are in nursing homes grooving on 'Back in the USSR'?"

"Singing 'The Long and Winding Road' each night when they turn out the lights," Katherine said.

"Ah yes, perfect," Lawrence agreed. "And serenading the pretty nurses with 'Yesterday.'" He began singing the first verse.

I was looking at Katherine when Lawrence called to me. "What's the best exit, Terry?"

We drove the length of Congress Street. Among the Christmas shoppers in the square I saw two men in rags pushing a shopping cart piled with trash bags. Something ran through me. Impulsively, I leaned toward the window and watched them fall away behind us.

"Take a right up here," I called to Lawrence. Another right, and two blocks later we were waiting in line at the parking garage. When we took our ticket I recognized the man in the booth as the fellow on duty the night Warren had brought me here.

As soon as we reached the second level I saw them waiting in the shadows. I asked Lawrence to stop. "Just for a minute," I said. I got out and walked straight toward them.

Charles was standing off by himself, shifting his weight from foot to foot to keep warm. Staring at me, I thought. Then I knew it was the limo he was looking at.

"I need to hire some people," I said to him. "Would any of you like to work for good wages."

"How much?" a young man with a gash on his forehead asked.

"Ten dollars an hour. More if you work hard."

I put out my hand to Charles. He didn't hesitate to shake it.

"Can I bring a few guys with me?"

"Anybody you can find," I said. His face was drawn and the gray beard made him look like an ancient mariner. Still, there was a quickness in his manner that fit perfectly my memory of him bounding down the hospital corridor in a Santa Claus outfit. "I'll pick you up here at seven tomorrow morning, is that all right?"

"Yes," he said. "Thanks."

"Thank you," I said. "I can use the help."

He never asked me what he would be doing or where he would be working. I heard the younger man asking him who I was as I walked away.

"I've got thirty roofs to shovel," I explained when I got back in the limo.

"Lawrence and I should help," Katherine said.

"Too cold for me," Lawrence said. "I know how to polish silver, though?"

There was a moment in the limousine, after the show. Katherine had taken off her necklace, a single strand of pearls, and given it to Olivia to hold. The child placed the necklace in my hands and then sat down beside me and rested her head on my shoulder. This surprised me, and I was self-conscious at first, sitting up straight and then sliding down in my seat as if I'd never sat in a car before. I saw Katherine smiling at this. I watched her taking the braid out of her hair. When she leaned across the space dividing us and kissed Olivia, her hair brushed my hand. "You have a new friend," she said, looking up at me.

By the time we reached the cottage Olivia was asleep. I carried her inside, up the stairs to the pale blue bedroom where her encyclopedias were in stacks on the floor. The moment I laid her down on the bed in front of the window she woke up and cried out. "My C book," she said desperately.

"I'll find it," I said. "It's right here."

It took me a while. When I placed it in her hands she thanked me.

"Olivia?" I said, and she smiled at me. "Do you know what your mommy looks like?"

Her smile never changed. "No," she said, "I don't see Mommy."

I said good night to her. She was opening the pages of the encyclopedia. The book that would accompany her through the dark night. At the door I turned back and said, "You have a beautiful mommy, Olivia."

She looked up at the ceiling. "I know I do," she said.

3 4

I will remember this, I thought, as the gate to Rose Point swung open and Charles Halworth bowed his head, gazing at the floor of the car. He would not look out the window. For as long as I live I will remember the way he closed his eyes and bowed his head. A kind of surrender, I thought.

He said nothing. Neither did the two men who came along with him to work for me. I had stopped at the hardware store for shovels. The three of them were dressed inadequately for the bitter cold morning, but in the hardware store I could buy them only gloves and hats. I made one last stop at Dunkin' Donuts where they were selling a special Christmas thermos. I bought three, and filled them with black coffee.

For the first part of the morning I worked with them on the roof of the Eldredge place. I was never more than ten feet from Charles, watching him, waiting for him to say something to me. He shoveled with his head down, plowing through the drifts with powerful strokes. Just once I saw him pause, stand up straight, and gaze across the point. A moment later he was back to work.

At noon we moved the ladders to the next cottage. I told the men that I would be back to pay them before dark and to drive them into town.

I looked at them. Charles nodded his head and began climbing. I watched a moment. The rubber sole of one sneaker was flapping loosely. His thin khaki pants were mended with strips of duct tape. What was it about me, I wondered angrily, that still believed I could fix his life? This man didn't want his life to be fixed, yet I believed I could sit with him tonight in my father's shop and tell him the daughter he lost was here, just down the road, with a limousine for him to ride in from now on.

I'm a fool, I thought, as I turned away. Somewhere along the way during my years in Hollywood I had lost my sense of what was real.

"I found these life jackets," Katherine said, when she greeted me on the beach. Olivia held a clamshell that the dog was trying to take from her hand.

The life jackets were the old orange stuffed ones that hung over your chest. "My girlfriend at camp used to call them Mae Wests," Katherine said. "I was out of college before I knew what she meant. I've lived a sheltered life." She put a life jacket on Olivia, but when she tried to tie her own, the canvas straps were twisted in back and they wouldn't reach around her.

"Let me help," I said. I stood behind her, still reeling

from the realization that my view of everything might be completely unreliable. Her hair smelled like apples, and I felt the warmth of her skin. When I finished I knelt down in front of Olivia to tie her straps. I saw her eyes clearly for the first time, cloudy pools of white with just a trace of brown. Floating eyes, unattached. Without light or a spark of recognition.

"You must tell Terry what you read last night, Teapot," Katherine said to her.

"Canada," the child, said brightly. "And guess what, Terry?"

I loved hearing her say my name, and I wondered if she remembered me holding her last night, and if I had won her trust. "What is it, Olivia?" I asked.

"They skate on ice in Canada. Like the ice you made for me and Mommy."

She smiled with pleasure. When I looked at Katherine she had the same smile. "Maybe Santa Claus will bring you some skates," I said.

"Santa Claus isn't real," Olivia said, with a serious expression. "He's a story, right, Mommy?"

"A lovely story," Katherine said. "But not real, you're right."

I guess I thought that the myth of Santa Claus was something parents worked dutifully to preserve when their kids were small, and I wondered if the mother of a blind child was under some obligation to play by different rules. No time for illusions, I thought.

"I think we'll send Lawrence shopping for skates today," Katherine said. "We'll get a pair for you too, Terry."

"I don't skate, I'm afraid," I told her.

"I'll teach you," she said.

Of course, I thought. Her father taught her. The teacher vanishes, but the lesson remains.

We got under way. If the sea had been anything but flat calm I would have tried to talk them out of this trip in a boat so small. The dog laid his head on Olivia's knees.

"As still as a mill pond," Katherine said, as she gazed toward Pumpkin Island.

I rowed us through a cathedral of silence. Seals popped their heads up through the water like submarine periscopes. Gulls were circling overhead. "So peaceful," I heard her say. Then she began singing to her daughter. "There'll be blue birds over the white cliffs of Dover, tomorrow, just you wait and see. When the world is free. Just you wait and see."

Halfway out Katherine pointed back to shore. "Look, you can see the men on the roof."

I turned.

"What men?" Olivia asked.

"Terry has some nice men shoveling snow from the roof of a big green cottage," her mother said.

"Why?" she asked.

I explained that it was the weight of the snow.

"But snow's not heavy, is it?" Olivia asked.

"Only when there's a lot of it," I said. "I should have had lunch for them. I forgot about that."

"When we get back we'll feed them a proper lunch," Katherine said. "Lawrence has the kitchen stocked for an army." She asked me if the men had worked for me before.

I told her they hadn't. "I haven't spent much time here," I said.

"Such a beautiful place," she said. "I can't believe my mother's had the cottage locked up my whole life."

"It's yours now," I said. "You can come back whenever you wish."

"It hasn't sunk in yet," she said. "Could we live here year round, do you think?"

I told her she would need to put some kind of heat in the cottage. "And you'd have to insulate all the pipes. But you could do it. It gets lonely here, though."

She hugged Olivia. "We never get lonely, do we, Teapot? We'll spend our days building igloos and making snow angels. How does that sound?"

"But Mommy," she replied, "what about all my friends in New York City?"

"We'd make new friends here in Maine. Terry's our new friend already."

"Would you live here with us, Terry?" Olivia asked. "We have twelve big bedrooms!"

"You do, that's right."

"And you should be staying with us," Katherine said. "Unless you're staying in your father's shop to be close to his spirit."

"Where is your father?" the child asked.

I almost said he was in heaven, but then I caught myself. Why would a child who didn't believe in Santa Claus believe in heaven.

"Terry lost his father," Katherine said.

"We lost my father too," Olivia said. "And we'll never see him again, will we, Mommy?"

I could tell that Katherine was uncomfortable with this question. "I lost my father, too," she said, taking Olivia's fists from her eyes again. "And look at Jack here. He lost his mother *and* his father."

"But he found us!" Olivia exclaimed.

"Yes, he did."

At the mention of his name, the dog swung his head toward Katherine, pushing his nose against her hand until she patted him. "It's no wonder dogs try so hard to please," she said. "They begin their lives as orphans, taken from their mothers."

All my life I'd been around dogs, and never once had I thought of them as orphans. But from now on they will always be orphans to me. Maybe the force of beauty is contained in its ability to surprise us. This is what drew me close to Katherine in our first hours together. If you can fall in love with someone for the things they say, then I was already in love with her.

35

In twenty minutes we were there. When the bottom of the boat slid onto the beach, Katherine looked up. "I feel like the Swiss family Robinson," she said. She tried to stand, but with Olivia draped over her knees, she couldn't move.

I held my arms out to her, forgetting that she couldn't see me. "May I lift you out, Olivia?" I asked her.

She looked up at me, smiling like she had won something. "Lift me, Terry," she said, eagerly.

I saw Katherine watching us. When our eyes met, she looked away. "Go! Run!" she shouted to Jack. He jumped to his feet and charged past us, heading off to explore the island.

"If he were a person," she said, "he'd be late for work every day, he'd leave his clothing all over the house, and he'd spend his weekends lying in bed, reading supermarket magazines. Crumbs on the pillowcases."

"If I were a dog," I said, "I'd hope to find a little girl just like you, Olivia."

"Blind like me?" she asked.

Again I saw Katherine looking at me. This time when I looked into her eyes she didn't turn away.

"Exactly like you," I said to Olivia.

Katherine took her daughter's hand. She told her that there were slippery rocks on the shore and that she would have to hold her hand tightly. Then she said, "And now we get to find out if your grandmother was telling us the truth."

There were only three trees on the Island, and it took us just a few minutes to find what Katherine was searching for. I held Olivia again while her mother got down on her knees and dug away the snow. It was below the third tree that we found a round stone set in the frozen ground, with these words carved into its face: "Our Beloved Friend, Sally."

She placed Olivia's hands on the stone and helped her trace the letters.

"I asked my mother why I should believe her," Katherine said, "after all these years of keeping this place hidden from me. Don't get me wrong, she's not a bad person, but there have been a lot of lies in my family. Lies about love, mostly. And when she told me about the cottage, I didn't believe her. I asked her why she hadn't told me before, and she said because she was always going to sell the place. Every year on New Year's Day she told herself that this would be the year she finally let the place go.

But then, she never followed through. It wasn't that she ever planned on coming back, but I think she wanted me to have the cottage. Some part of her wanted me to come here with my own children. The part of her that isn't made of slate."

It began snowing while we walked together across the center of the Island. When we got to an open field, Katherine hooked the leash to Jack's collar and placed the other end in Olivia's hand. "You and Jack can walk here," she said. And then to the dog, "Take your girl for a stroll."

Somehow the dog knew to move cautiously. We followed behind. Their footprints lay ahead of us in the snow. I listened to Katherine talk about her life. I felt her leaning closer to me, her voice becoming more familiar and calm. She told me that she had been working as a social worker in New York when someone told her about a blind baby whose parents had left her when she was only a few weeks old.

"When I first met her she was nine months and had been in four foster homes already. Have you spent time around babies, Terry?"

"Never," I said.

"Well, any mother will tell you that there's a magical time at nine months. The baby has learned how to sleep through the night, and how to eat, and to sit up. It's amazing. With feet still small enough to wash in a teacup, and yet smiling at you and making intelligent sounds to try to communicate. You want to freeze time at nine months, Terry. I fell in love, and I couldn't give her away."

We stopped and watched Olivia making a snowball. When she finished, she threw it up into the air and the dog caught it in his mouth.

"And she's been a gift to me," Katherine went on. "Olivia has taught me to live in the present. That's a *great* gift, you know? She's made me a better person."

I waited a moment, then told her she and Olivia were both lucky. "You have each other," I said.

She didn't seem to hear this. "I already told you that I was the kid in my neighborhood who broke everything," she said. "Well, I grew into a young woman in a broken family. And then my engagement was broken. And now I'm a mother with a broken child." She laughed at herself. "I never thought of this before," she said.

It was snowing harder when we made our way back to the shore. The wind was stronger as well. Olivia was in her mother's arms. When we reached the top of a bluff I was shocked to see that the passage between us and the Point had disappeared in fog and blowing snow.

"Where did *that* come from?" I said. "We have to go, we have to hurry now, Katherine."

I took Olivia from her and we ran down the shore. We followed our footprints in the snow. They led us to where the boat had been, but the tide had turned while we were exploring the island, and the boat was gone. We stood at the edge of the water looking for it through the dizzying snow. The sea was no longer calm; there were strong waves breaking on the beach.

"The tide took it," I said, miserably. "My damn fault."

At last Katherine spotted it, maybe thirty feet out. I took off my boots as quickly as I could. When I looked out again, the boat had vanished. It had been there, ghostlike in the blowing snow, then it was gone.

"There, Terry," Katherine shouted.

I kept it in sight this time. I heard her telling me to be careful as I waded into the frigid water. The beach fell off sharply beneath my feet. I swam only a few strokes before my arms turned to lead. From then on I had to force my mind to concentrate and my legs to keep kicking.

It seemed to take forever to reach the boat, and when I grabbed hold of it to try and pull myself up, I couldn't tighten my grip enough to keep from slipping off. It took several tries before I was able to drape my arms over the stern, first one, then the other with great effort. I saw the seawater run off my coat sleeves and make a puddle in the bottom of the boat. I closed my eyes and tried again to tell myself what I needed to do to turn the boat around and bring it back to the island. I could hear Katherine calling my name. I tried to call back to her but my jaw was nearly frozen shut, and all I could do was make a sound above a shallow groan. There was a pounding in my head, and when I looked down at my hands I saw they were a deep shade of red, as if they had been scalded. *Just kick,* I told myself. *Keep kicking until you turn the boat around.* I could barely feel my legs or my feet, but I heard the sound of their movement in the water, and slowly the bow began to turn. I was shaking violently and my eyes were closed when I felt the shore under my knees and someone taking hold of me.

"Here we are," I heard Katherine say very softly, as if there was nothing to fear. "Here we are, Olivia, you're going to help me get Terry into the boat now."

I opened my eyes and saw their hands on my arms. "Still snowing," I said.

"Lovely, isn't it, Terry?" Katherine said. "We're going to make our way back to Rose Point now."

They lifted and pushed me until I was on the floor of the boat. Then Katherine made the dog lie next to me. She pushed the dog's head down against my face and I felt the warmth of its fur. "Stay just like that, Jack," she said. Then, as she began to row, she said, "there, Terry, Jack will warm you up."

The child said, "Jack is always warm, right, Mommy?" I didn't hear her mother respond. Instead I heard a strange ticking sound that I could not place at first, but which I tried to stop. I heard Olivia asking what the sound was, and I tried to apologize.

"Terry's teeth are chattering," I heard Katherine say. "I'll row and we'll let Terry just chatter away."

She rowed us steadily through the black waves. "We don't have far to go," she said. "We'll all take nice hot baths when we get home. We'll have hot chocolate. I'll make us all brownies."

"What about Jack?" Olivia called out.

"Gravy and potatoes for Jack," Katherine said.

As we neared the point the wind grew even stronger. I saw the blowing spray off the whitecaps washing across their faces. I watched Katherine working the oars, turning us from side to side to keep us steady in the churning waves. The water in the bottom of the boat had now risen up their red boots.

I listened to Katherine scold her mother for not keeping a bowline on the boat, and then herself for not taking the time to tie one on. And then she shouted to someone. "Oh yes!" she said. "There's someone to help us."

I heard her yelling "Thank you. Thank you, sir." Suddenly I saw Charles Halworth's face. And then his arms as he lifted Olivia out of the boat and onto his shoulders. I understood then what was happening. The waves were crashing behind us and it was only a matter of time, seconds, before a wave would lift up the back of the boat and flip us over.

"Keep rowing," I heard Charles telling Katherine.

He had the bow of the boat against his chest and was walking backward. Only his shoulders and head were above the water. Each time a wave ran beneath us from behind and raised the back of the boat, he lifted the front to hold us flat.

We were safely on the beach when Charles lifted me from the boat and laid me in the sand. I looked up and saw his face. Saltwater had turned his lips white. Beside him, Katherine was holding Olivia and looking down at me. "He saw us from the roof, Terry," she said. "How will we ever thank you?"

It was only a moment. The three of them together. Finally together. Three people who shared the same soul had somehow traveled across time and were standing together on this shore. Though none of them knew it.

"Up we go," Charles said. He lifted me onto his back. I heard him tell me to talk to him and I tried, but I was slipping away. The last thing I remember was the fear that the moment had passed us by, that this group of three would now scatter in different directions, never to find one another again.

36

I was in a bedroom in the cottage with Lawrence. He had taken off my clothes, wrapped me in blankets, and put me in a stuffed chair in front of a roaring fire.

"Katherine wants me to get you in the tub," he said.

"Not now," I told him. "Let me sit here. But where's Charles?"

"Who?"

"The man who helped us," I said.

"He's downstairs with the others. I gave him some of my clothes. They want me to drive them back to the city."

I thought of the hotel room. "Lawrence, can you bring him up here, please? I need to tell him something."

He left to get him. I looked into the fire and tried to piece together what had happened, how I'd gotten here. I remembered Charles taking me out of the boat and laying me in the sand.

"He's driving us back," I heard someone say.

I turned and saw Charles in the doorway.

"Are you okay?" I asked him.

"Yes," he said. "The others wanted me to ask for our

money. I told them we could wait if you can't pay us now. Are you going to be all right?"

I looked into his eyes and thanked him. "I want to pay you," I said. "There's money in the shop. It's in the drawer below the workbench."

"I don't think I can do that."

"Yes, it's fine. Take enough. Whatever you need. I mean, it doesn't matter."

"You'll have to tell me how much, sir," he said.

"Okay. A hundred for each of you. Would that be enough?"

"More than enough. Thank you." He turned to leave.

"No, wait, please. Do you remember the man who was the caretaker here?"

He nodded. "I knew the man," he said.

"I know you did," I said to him. He was looking right at me then. "I'm his son."

He didn't turn away.

I told him that he had been gone a long time. He just looked down at the floor. "So have I," I said. "But we've both come back."

I told him that I had a room he could stay in. "The Regency Hotel," I said. "There's a room key in the same drawer with the money, in the shop. You can stay there."

He didn't look up from the floor.

"It's a nice room," I said. "Stay there. You'll be comfortable."

He took a deep breath, then raised his head. "Thank you," he said, "but I can't take handouts."

"Think of it as a repayment, then, for saving my life."

He thought about this. "Could my friends use it?"

"Whatever you want," I said. "I left your name at the front desk," I said.

"My name?" he said.

"Charles Halworth," I said.

It took a moment before he spoke again. "I think you took my fingerprints once," he said.

"A long time ago," I said.

"I'd forgotten," he said.

"Are you sure?" I asked him.

"No," he said, "I never forgot." He lowered his eyes again.

"I never forgot either," I said.

He glanced out into the hallway. When he looked back at me, he said, "I won't be back tomorrow."

"I could use your help."

"I'm sorry," he said.

"You don't have to be sorry," I told him. "I'm glad you were here today."

He left then. I listened to him going down the stairs. I thought of going after him. I could hear Katherine and Olivia below me. If I never saw him again, I knew I would never forgive myself for letting him leave. But what would *he* want, I wondered. What would he want me to do? I thought back over everything that Warren and Callie had told me, and I decided that I couldn't say anything until I spoke with him again and told him the truth.

Lawrence came upstairs again. "He asked me to go into your shop for him. He doesn't want to get the money himself."

"Fine," I said. "In the drawer below the workbench. And the key. There's a key there for room 603 in the Regency Hotel. Can you take him there, please?"

"Done," he said. "Get your bath. You look awful."

3 7

I don't know how long I slept in the chair in front of the fire. When I awoke the house was quiet and I could feel my legs again. I got to my feet slowly. When I turned, I saw Katherine and Olivia asleep on the bed behind me. The dog was on the floor. His tail flew up for a second, but other than this, he remained perfectly still. A resigned look was in his dark eyes, as if this were part of his supervisory job, to guard them, and to wait patiently for them to return from wherever it was they went in their sleep.

Olivia was wearing white tights under a crimson-colored velvet dress that was covered in dog hairs. Her mother wore a matching dress and blue wool tights. The black braid of her hair fell over her left shoulder onto her breast. What was curious about them was that, though they were asleep, they didn't seem to be resting. It was as if their sleep had not carried them away from the concerns of the waking world.

When I stepped closer to them, the dog raised his head in anticipation. For a moment I had a sense that I belonged here and that I had traveled across a vast emptiness to stand in this room with them.

The day was almost over, the last of the sea light lay in a ribbon across the room's yellow-painted wainscoting. I was looking at Katherine when she opened her eyes. "I came upstairs to help you get a bath," she whispered. "But you were sleeping."

"I'm fine," I said. "I'm warm."

"No," she said, "you need a bath."

She insisted. She got off the bed slowly, without waking Olivia. I followed her down the hallway, looking at her hand and wanting to take it in mine.

She went into the bathroom ahead of me, closed the door behind us, and began drawing the water. "I'm going to sit outside the door," she said.

When the tub was full and I had turned off the water, I heard her call to me in a low voice.

"I forgot to tell you we have pink water," she said. "Very stylish."

I told her it was the rust that had collected in the old cast-iron pipes. "The pipes were drained for thirty years," I told her. "I helped my father close this place. I was eight years old. Kennedy had just been assassinated." Perhaps I had gone too far. I waited, trying not to move, or make a sound that would prevent me from hearing her.

"On the Cape we always drain our pipes in the summer house by Columbus weekend."

"It was Christmas," I told her. "Your mother wanted *Serenity* opened for Christmas."

"She came here for Christmas? That sounds too sentimental for my mother."

I thought of her father in the room at the hotel tonight. Warm beneath the blankets. How I could drive Katherine there. Knock on the door and put an end to all the secrets. What kept me from doing this was just a pledge to the man's brother. But surely I could explain my way out of that. I could tell Warren that I had said something to Katherine, something without thinking, and then the story had unraveled.

"I just remember the empty rooms," I told her. "So many empty rooms. It seemed a shame to me."

"So you never saw my mother then?"

"No," I lied. "Only the cottage, opening it, and then closing it down. Did she tell you why she never came back?"

"Bad memories," she said. "The memory of my father here before he left her."

"Well, you have the place now," I said. "You can make your own memories."

"Yes. I have to get used to that. And to the fact that my father was here, in these rooms. Most of my life I've been all right with this, I mean, without knowing my father. Actually, I had surrogate fathers. My mother's husbands, all of them very nice, we got along very well. One of them took me to Disney World when I was seven or eight. I had a good childhood and I shouldn't complain."

"You don't sound like you're complaining."

"Well, thank you. When I found Olivia, that was when I began to miss my father. I just wanted to show her to him, and for the first year we were together I had the feeling that I was going to find him, somewhere. I was going to walk down a street and there he would be. Of course, that was silly."

I wondered if her mother had anticipated this and had held onto *Serenity* for Katherine. I told her this.

"No," she said. "And I think if Olivia had been a normal child, she never would have told me about this place. Last summer we spent some time with her on the Cape. She has a mansion there. A very big social life that we kept interfering with. We were in the way from the moment we arrived. I don't think she was doing it on purpose, but she kept leaving things laying around on the floor, and Olivia kept falling over them."

I heard her breathe deeply. A sigh. Steam from my bath had turned to frost on the inside of the windowpanes.

I told her that Olivia would grow to love Rose Point. "She'll be safe here," I said.

"That's the thing all parents want, isn't it?"

"I wouldn't know," I said.

"Yes, you would, Terry," she insisted. "When you look back to your own childhood and remember your father and mother, you can see that all parents want to be able to protect their children. Nothing else matters as much as that."

"And what do you get in return?" I asked.

"Many things. You'll see for yourself some day."

"I don't know," I said, "the time is flying past."

"Well, you shouldn't miss out on being a father. I can tell you'll be very good at it. You wonder sometimes," she said, softly. "I wasn't going to have children. I mean, my fiancé and I had an understanding about that. You know, no kids to interrupt us reading the *New York Times* each morning. Our lives were, well, you could say that our lives were . . . orderly. I guess that's the word. But a couple of other words come to mind as well. Predictable. Empty."

"Lots of people live empty lives," I said.

"Now, looking back, empty is the most accurate word," she said, as though she hadn't heard me. "I think about it a lot. In New York there are so many old women living alone. I watch them. And though they are alone, they make a great effort to present themselves well. You can see past their deprivation, you can catch a glimpse from time to time of their elegance. In a simple gesture, I mean. The way one might raise her hand, or turn her head. So completely alone in the world now, and yet once they had whole lives. And if they were mothers, then they were once the center of someone's attention. I guess whenever I'm feeling sorry for myself, I watch them, and I feel lucky. Because once you're a mother in this world, no one can ever take that from you. You can lose everything else, but never the memory of once being adored. You have that to carry with you, to the end."

What she said made me feel better about my own mother, and I told her this.

"Your mother had her little boy," she said. "And she got to live near this beautiful place. But you should have taken her sailing, Terry McQuinn. No excuses for not learning how to sail. I must have sailed here with my mother. I wish I could remember."

"Did she teach you?" I asked her.

"Yes. I can remember her painting her nails in the boat while she shouted commands at me." She laughed a moment. "Of the things I know how to do, Terry, sailing is the one talent I believe I will be able to use in the next world. I must take you sailing here someday."

I waited for the next thing she would tell me. Outside the window there was the moonlight across the tops of the trees. I thought how impossible the odds were that I would ever be taking a bath at Rose Point.

When she didn't say anything, I was afraid she would leave. "I want you to know why I came back," I said.

"Back?"

"Yes, after driving to the airport in the storm."

"You came back because the airport was closed," she said innocently. "You already told me."

"It wasn't just that," I said. I looked at my hands. There was soft white flesh around the stitches on my thumb. My words echoed in the room. "I could have spent the night at the airport," I said, "but I had given a ride to this man, a traveling salesman. He was selling Torahs."

"Really?" she said.

"Yes, door-to-door. And he told me that in the Torah there's a passage asking us how differently we would live a single day if we knew in advance that it was our last day. You reminded me of this when you were telling me how Olivia has taught you to live in the present tense."

"How do you live?" she asked.

"The future, always," I confessed. "You are only as good as your next deal." There was a long pause, and I decided to say something I knew I wouldn't be able to retract. "This is the future too," I said. "Being here with you."

She said she didn't understand.

"I know," I said. "You never knew it, but I've been waiting a long time for this, and looking for you." There was a faint movement outside the door. I held my hands out in front of me in the bath and they were shaking a little.

"Where?" she asked softly. "Where have you been looking for me, Terry?"

"Everywhere," I said.

There was only silence. I tried to picture her expression. Then I heard a sound somewhere. "It's Olivia," Katherine said. "I'll be right back."

I waited maybe an hour for her, but she never returned. I wrapped the blankets around me and opened the bathroom door. From the hallway I could hear Katherine reading to Olivia in their bedroom. And I knew she had forgotten me.

3 8

I left the cottage quietly. The only thing I wanted was to find Charles in the hotel and sit and talk with him. Tell him everything before this night was over. I drove into the city, going over the sentences in my mind. How would I begin? Well, I didn't know *how*, but maybe I thought he'd shake my hand and put his arm around me and tell me everything was going to work out fine for everyone.

I continued to rehearse the lines until I was standing outside the door to the room. Right up to the second I pushed it open and saw that it was empty. No one had been here since I'd filled the bureau drawers and the closet with new clothes.

I looked at the three paintings on the wall. And the shining brass lamps. I turned the light off and saw the lights from the Christmas tree in the square reflected in the dark window. I walked across the room, opened the window, and I pushed it as high as it would go and looked down into the square. A man with a white apron over his coat was selling coffee from a cart. Someone from the Salvation Army stood behind a black kettle ringing a bell.

Something came over me. Anger at myself. And defiance. Not wanting to run away again, or to lose the things I cared about. Not wanting to let go of the illusions that had colored my life. Mostly, not wanting to give up on the immense feeling of possibility. I started by dropping a pair of new socks out the window. I watched them float to the ground where they landed in a stand of thin birch trees that had been strung with white lights. After that first one I dropped all seven pairs of socks to the ground, each of them sort of sailing across the dark sky for a few moments before they fell into the square. People were looking up at me and I didn't care. I turned away from the window and quickly gathered up all of the remaining clothes, then headed for the door.

By the time I came out of the elevator and walked out the front doors of the hotel, the fight in me was gone and I allowed myself the humiliation of walking through the square with my head bowed as I picked up the socks. A policeman was watching me when I carried the whole bundle of clothing to the corner where the Salvation Army man was still ringing his bell. "Would you know someone who could use all this?" I asked him.

He nodded. "Of course," he said. "You can leave that with me."

I had forgotten over the years how soothing it was to work on something with your hands. Back in the shop that night I worked slowly on the wooden sled until it was finished, trying not to hurry or to think about how it was going to look. I just worked on what was in front of me until the day had drained out of me and I was tired enough to go to sleep.

In my sleep I had imagined making such a fine sled that Katherine and Olivia would keep it over the years and be reminded of me. But by morning when I gazed at the work I had done the night before, it fell far short of that. Warren stopped by when I was waxing the oak runners with a candle.

"You're still here," he said, walking to the workbench for a look at the sled. "Can Hollywood survive without you for this long?"

I didn't want to talk about that. "Your brother was here," I told him. "I found him in the city and hired him."

I don't know what reaction I expected from him. Anger perhaps. Instead he turned the sled over and ran his palm along one runner. "I spoke to him," he said. "I want to show you something."

We walked together until we saw Charles in the distance straddling the ridge of a snow-covered roof.

"He called me for a ride this morning," Warren told me. "The first thing he's asked me for in five years." He looked at me with an expression I couldn't interpret. He didn't say anything before he turned away and gazed at his brother.

"What do you want to say to me, Warren?" I asked him.

He shook his head slowly and told me he wasn't sure. I waited. Off in the harbor a flock of gulls followed a fishing boat through the channel, their flashing white wings, like a deck of cards thrown up into the sky.

"I just don't want anything to happen to him," he said, slowly. "I don't want to lose him. He was my brother long before he had anything to do with these people out here."

"Well," I said to him, "I think it's off to a good start."

"But how will it end, that's what concerns me."

"Maybe he's not going to run away anymore," I answered.

He took off his hat and one glove, then raked his hair back with his hand. "What happened out here yesterday?" he asked me.

I told him. "If he asks me again, I'm going to tell him," I said.

He looked into my eyes. "When your father told me that she was coming up here for Christmas, I asked if he knew what kind of person she had grown up to be. Of course, he didn't know. I guess I was worried that she might be like her mother. She might hurt him. Does that make sense?"

"I think she's a good person, Warren," I said.

He nodded his head. "Will you let me be the one to tell him?" he said.

"You're the only one who should tell him," I said.

39

I drove to town and bought Charles a steak sandwich for lunch. When I climbed up the ladder to give it to him, I saw that Warren had given him a rope that was tied around his waist and the base of a chimney for a safety line. He told me that he wasn't hungry.

"Well," I said, "you have to eat."

He stopped and looked at me. "What do you remember?" he asked.

"Everything," I said.

He thought about this a moment. "Your father found a diamond earring," he said.

"I know."

"Those kids in the hospital?"

"I remember them too," I said.

Finally I got him to take the sandwich and coffee. He sat down on the roof, leaning his back against the chimney, and asked me about my father. "What kind of father was he to you?"

I wasn't sure how to answer that question, so instead I

told him the first thing that came into my mind. "When I was little," I recalled, "he kept his nails and screws in old baby-food jars, attached to an overhead shelf by their lids. Every man in America in that generation did the same thing. And he had his army stuff in a trunk in the basement. I remember a canteen. A folding shovel, for digging your foxhole, and this heavy coat that dragged behind me when I marched around. He let me play with this stuff. Eventually I lost all of it . . . you know, scattered around at friends' houses."

Remembering these things made me realize that in those years my father had been younger than I was now. I'd never thought of this before. I had always been too self-centered to see him from that perspective.

"Listen," I said to Charles. "Do you want to call it a day?"

He stood up quickly and said he wanted to keep working.

"Do you know the story about the people who owned this cottage?" he asked me. "The Rideouts?"

"The name is familiar," I told him.

"They threw this dinner party once and hired the chef from the Plaza Hotel in New York to do the cooking. Your poor father had to drive him up and back."

I smiled at him. "I wonder what the two of them talked about for eight hours," I said.

"Rich people, probably," he said.

I felt like he and I were getting close to something, so I asked him if he'd ever come back here after the accident.

"Yes," he said. Then he continued shoveling and I thought he wouldn't tell me anything more. But he stopped and went on. "For a few summers I came back here. I slept on people's boats in the harbor. I spent the days in the woods at the golf course. I was always hiding somewhere out here; I thought they might come back. I was foolish. I was here when the men came and cleaned out the cottage. I watched them fill two big trucks. I never came back after that."

I waited a moment, then told him I had met Callie. "You could see this place from the hospital," I said.

He said something, but I couldn't make it out. "Why didn't you stay with Callie?" I said. "She loved you. Why should she have to go through her life thinking you're dead?"

He stopped again, leaned his shovel against the chimney, and looked at me. "She deserved someone better than me," he said.

"Well, she never found anyone," I told him. "And who were you to decide that, anyway?"

This was all he wanted to say to me. I watched him pick up his shovel and start in again. Before I left him I said one last thing. I told him I thought he had been kicking himself long enough.

I imagined him watching us later that afternoon when we went sledding on the snow-covered dunes behind the yacht club. We posted Lawrence in his new L.L. Bean boots at the bottom of the hill to catch Olivia. Katherine and I ran alongside the sled. "Again!" Olivia shouted as soon as the sled came to a stop. "Again, Terry!"

Her mother and I pulled her up the hill until she decided that she could do this on her own. She took the rope from Katherine and marched ahead of us to the top. Anyone passing by would scarcely take note of us, I thought. Four people on the side of a white hill. Just a normal family enjoying a winter afternoon.

Katherine and I rode with Olivia for the last run of the day, and the three of us landed in a heap, in each other's arms, laughing and holding onto one another. If Charles Halworth had been watching us from the roof where he was shoveling, I wondered if he would think we belonged together.

Katherine brushed the snow off my hair and told me she was sorry.

"For what?" I asked.

"Last night," she said. "I started reading with Olivia and I forgot. I'm sorry." She took my hand.

Olivia and Jack walked ahead of us. "A long time ago I read about a man in England," she said. "It was the summer of 1453, the beginning of the summer, and he locked himself in his room. He spent every day in his room. The whole summer. No one knew what he was doing, and no one could get him to come out. His wife was certain that he'd lost his mind. She took the children and ran away. In September he came out with a telescope that he had built. He'd spent every day and night the whole summer cutting and polishing mirrors. And that fall he discovered the planet Uranus in the night sky."

She stopped walking and turned to face me. "I'm not even sure it's a true story, but it's what I think about sometimes. I mean, I feel like I've made this world for Oliva and me, a small world where we hide. And I hope that we'll discover something there. Something that will make life better for her. But sometimes, Terry, I feel like we live in two places. Do you ever feel that this life is only a shadow of another that we live in some other place, somewhere above us? And every so often when the two come together we catch a glimpse of the real meaning of our lives."

"What's it like," I asked her, "in those moments when the two come together?"

She smiled at me and looked around us. "Like this, Terry," she said. "Moments like this when we don't need anything more than what is right here, all around us."

Like this, I thought, looking into her eyes. I realized how close our faces were. I didn't move. I drank in her attention, her closeness, thinking that maybe I had done something right to earn her touch. She smiled for a moment, then closed her eyes and kissed me.

"Maybe I shouldn't have done that," she said.

"No," I told her. "It was the right thing to do."

"Are you sure?"

"I'm sure."

40

We had dinner together that night, the four of us in candlelight at the dining room table. We sang some carols in front of the fireplace until it was time for Katherine to get Olivia into her pajamas. Before they went upstairs she said that I had to stay for dessert. "I made a pumpkin pie," she said. "And I need volunteers to eat it."

I helped Lawrence with the dishes, then told him I was going to take a walk.

"You'll be back?" he said.

"For my pie," I said. But when I was outside I decided to go back to the shop. I didn't want to intrude on Olivia's time with her mother. And I wanted to think about all that had happened that day.

I dried the sled and put on another coat of varnish before I got into bed. I was almost asleep when Katherine knocked on the door. She stood in the doorway of the shop, holding something in her hands.

"Don't you like pumpkin pie?" she asked.

When I turned on the light I saw something in her eyes.

She wore a light blue sweater and jeans. Her hair was
down on her shoulders.

I started to get up.

"No, that's okay," she said, "I'll just leave it here."

"Don't go," I said. "I'm not tired enough to sleep, anyway." I sat up with the blanket around me. I waited until
she turned around, then I put my pants and shirt on.

"I've got two plastic forks here," I said to her.

I turned on the radio and we sat on the bed eating her
pie in the dim light. One piece had been cut and she told
me that she had tested the pie on Lawrence first.

"He survived," she said. "But he's got a cast-iron stomach."

"So have I," I said.

She told me that she and Olivia had enjoyed the sledding.
"I can't believe you built the sled right here," she said.

"That's the absolute limit of my carpentry skills," I told
her. "Anything that doesn't fall apart an hour after I build
it is a miracle. If my father were here he could have made
you a much better sled in one fifth of the time."

I told her that I had put on another coat of varnish. "I'll
bring it by in the morning," I said.

"I think we'll leave it in the cottage so it's always here
when we come," she said.

I thought of Charles's things that my father had
returned to the cottage before he died. It made me wish I
could see his face again.

An old song by Roy Orbison came on the radio. When Katherine told me that it was one of her favorites, I asked her to stand up. I took her in my arms and we danced. After a few moments she laid her head on my shoulder. I felt her breath on my face. "I have to tell you something, Terry," she said.

"What is it?"

"I'm not a person who thinks about things as deeply as I should. I keep busy; I don't dwell on things. But since I've been here I've realized something about myself. There's a great amount of loneliness in me. When you have this inside you, you don't let anyone get too close, because if you come to need them or to love them and they leave, then there will be too much loneliness in your heart. So you push people away. I've become good at that. I pushed everybody away until I found Olivia, the one person who wouldn't leave me. She'll always stay with me. At least that's what I've told myself from the day I brought her home. Only now, I see how wrong that is." She looked right at me, into my eyes. "I feel like I can trust you, Terry. You won't add to the loneliness. And when I kissed you today I knew what I wanted for my daughter. I want her to fall in love someday and have a full life. And this means that I must help her become strong enough to leave me."

I listened until she was finished and the room was silent around us. I looked up at my mother's photograph and she seemed to be staring at me. I told Katherine that Olivia would always be with her, no matter where her life took her. "Remember," I said, "you told me about the old women in the city, the ones who were once loved by a child?"

She raised her head and I saw that she was smiling. "Yes," she said. "So, if you come into the city some day and see me crossing the street with my cane and those black shoes with the old lady heels, you'll remind me?"

"I will," I said.

Early the next morning Lawrence drove the limousine to the shop, where I was waiting for him. "Katherine and Olivia are sleeping," he said to me, when I got in beside him. "And by the way, I saw your man earlier this morning. He was standing in the snow, just staring at the skating rink you built. He's a handsome man despite his circumstances," he said. "It's Christmas Eve tomorrow. Maybe we should invite him for a nice dinner."

"I was thinking the same thing," I said.

"And what are we up to now?" he asked me.

"Trespassing," I said. "A surprise for Katherine."

"You mean she gets to bail us both out of jail?"

"Lawrence," I said, "you are looking at a man for whom indoor pools at hotels are not warm enough. But I am taking the queen's only daughter sailing."

"You didn't get enough saltwater up your nose on your little breathtaking excursion the other day?" he said. He looked at me with a wise expression. "You're trying, aren't you?"

"I'm trying, Lawrence," I said.

We went from cottage to cottage, looking in the windows of the carriage houses and the garages, the barns and the outbuildings, until we found a small sailboat on a trailer we could pull behind the limousine. I had my father's keys, but we didn't need one; the padlock on the door fell off in my hand.

We pulled the canvas tarp off the boat, revealing its flawless white hull and varnished mahogany seats. "I wonder how much this sweet little number costs," Lawrence said.

I ran my hand over the polished oak mast that lay along the deck, lashed at the bow and stern with cotton rope.

"Where's the steering wheel?" Lawrence asked.

We backed the limousine up to the front of the trailer, then tied one end of a rope around it. I got into the trunk with the other end.

As soon as we started down the lane I had to stand up in the trunk, place the soles of my boots against the inside of the bumper, and lean all my weight backward to keep the trailer from pulling free and rolling away behind us.

At the shore we backed it onto the beach beside the yacht club until the rear wheels of the limousine were under water. With one hard push the boat was floating freely off the trailer. I tied it to the dock and stood looking at a confusing mess of ropes and pulleys, wondering how we would ever rig it properly.

"What do you think, Lawrence?" I said. "Are we smart enough to figure this out together?"

"How many weeks do we have?" he said.

We set the mast without much trouble, but we had to leave the ropes and wire stays hanging hopelessly.

Driving back to the cottage, Lawrence asked me if he could sit out the sail. "Unless you need me for ballast," he said. "I'd rather baby-sit Olivia so she's spared another shipwreck."

"You'd rather baby-sit?" I said, smiling at him.

"You need all the help you can get, my friend," he said.

Katherine and Olivia were asleep on couches in the living room. I took Katherine's hand, and when she opened her eyes she smiled at me.

We walked to the yacht club, and just before the sailboat came into view I made her close her eyes and keep them closed until we were standing on the dock.

I saw her face light up. "Some assembly is required," I said.

"She's beautiful," she said.

We were underway in no time. The sea was calm, with barely enough wind to fill the sails. I was sitting in the bow, warming my hands in my pockets while Katherine stood at the tiller, steering us.

We followed the shoreline, and as we passed each cottage I told her everything I knew about the people who had lived here when I was a boy. I was surprised how

much I remembered. All the names came back to me, and
with them the stories my father had told around our dinner table. There was a woman named Potter who made a
trip to the bank in Ellsworth every Friday afternoon to fill
her purse with $20 bills that she distributed on Saturday
morning as tips to the waiters at the yacht club, the college
kids who worked at the tennis courts and the golf course.
"She also tipped my father each week," I told Katherine.
"Twenty dollars was a lot of money in those days. She was
in her nineties, and when she returned one summer nearly
blind, it became my father's job to drive her to the bank
every Friday for the twenty-dollar bills, and to walk her
around every Saturday morning."

I remembered the man named Phillips who insisted on
playing the golf course backward, starting each round on
the eighteenth hole and ending on the first. Katherine
laughed at this. And another old man named Chapman
who once tipped my father a hundred dollars for finding
his missing cuff link in the woodpile behind his cottage.

"My father laid the hundred dollar bill on the table
when he told my mother and me. I remember thinking
that we were suddenly rich."

A seal popped its head up just off our bow. The breeze
fell off to a slow sigh. "Wonderful stories," Katherine
said. "I'm so grateful to you."

I told her there were more. Mr. and Mrs. Jacobi, who
owned *The Gathering* cottage played the violin and viola

for the Wednesday night clam chowder suppers at the yacht club. They were survivors of a Nazi concentration camp, where they had been forced to play their instruments while their fellow prisoners were herded into the gas chambers.

"My father told us that each night, when they finished playing and people applauded, the old man would raise his hand for them to stop. He would apologize and say, 'Not so good. Not so good I play anymore.'"

"When your father told you these stories," Katherine said, "how did you feel?"

"Like an outsider," I said. "I guess as a boy I was fascinated. But when I got older, I had a lot of anger for these people."

She pulled in one of the ropes and cleated it down. "You wouldn't have liked me very much in those years either," she said.

"I don't know about that," I told her.

"No, I was from that privileged world. There was always a lot of money, and the things that money could buy. When I arrived at Mount Holyoke College there were a hundred girls who brought their horses to school with them."

"Yes," I told her, "that might have rubbed me the wrong way when I was a teenager. You know, I think the reason I hated these people out here was to keep from wanting what they had. But I wanted it anyway."

"Well," she said, "who could help but want it? And the farther you are from it, the greater its allure." She looked past me, out to the open ocean, and said that even now a part of her wanted to just sail away from everything. "Never come back," she said.

I heard the hopelessness in her voice. I moved close enough to her to take her hand. It felt like the most natural thing to do, and I didn't pause to consider the consequences. She looked into my eyes, then started to lean against me before she caught herself and pulled away.

"You're a good man," she said. "You mother and father raised a good son." She smiled at me, then turned away and sailed us back.

4 2

It was dark when we got back to the cottage. Lawrence was setting the table with Olivia. "I made BLTs," he said. "Enough to feed the search party that I was going to send out to look for you two."

We ate before a blazing fire in the dining room. I told them Hollywood stories until it was time for Katherine and Olivia to begin their nightly ritual. "Why don't we tell Terry how glad we are that he was here this Christmas," Katherine said to her daughter.

"I'm glad you were here with us," Olivia sang out.

"I have an idea," I said. "How about tonight I tell you a story?"

I looked to Katherine. She nodded her approval. "Mommy says it's fine," I told the child.

Before we went upstairs I remembered the bird's nest in the mailbox. We climbed all the stairs together to the widow's walk and sat beneath the Christmas tree. "I've never told a story to a child before. You're the first, Olivia." I placed the nest in her hands. It took a while for me to stop feeling self-conscious and to lose myself in

Olivia; that's the only way I can describe it. I let myself be drawn close enough to her that *I* didn't matter anymore, and then a story came into my head. The story of a bird named Sheila who lived in the mailbox and spent her days going from one mailbox to another and flying away with all the bad news. "The bills, of course, but also the sad letters," I told the child.

I went on and on effortlessly, sentence after sentence falling into place. There was a child who befriended the bird and who opened the lids on all the mailboxes on his way from school each day. The bird trusted the child and led him to where she kept all the sad letters. And they read them together and rewrote them, taking out all the sad parts and the mean things people had written that they really never meant to write, and writing the things that they wanted in their hearts to say, but somehow never got around to saying.

I heard Katherine's voice, and for a moment I didn't know where I was or where the voice was coming from.

"I want to know how it ends," Katherine said, softly. She leaned close to me and looked down at Olivia.

"I'm not sure," I told her. "Do I have to know the ending?"

She smiled at me. "No, maybe it's better without an ending," she said.

I thought again of how Olivia had taught her to live in the present. This moment, *right now,* is all we have.

Maybe this is the best way to live. Maybe a fulfilled life is just one beginning after another. No endings, just beginnings.

"Look," I heard Katherine say to me. "Look who's sleeping."

I looked down at Olivia. She was fast asleep. "Maybe tonight she should sleep," I said to Katherine. I saw the doubt in her eyes. "You'll have plenty of other nights to build your telescope," I said.

I carried Olivia down to the second floor. "She's always slept beside me," Katherine said. I waited for her to show me which room. "I have an idea," she said. "I'll be right back."

She went into another room and returned with blankets and a pillow. I watched her make a bed for Olivia in front of the windows, in the blue room with scallop shells stenciled in gold around the ceiling. She closed the door behind us. "Tell me," I said. "I've been meaning to ask you why she puts her fists against her eyes."

She took my hands and made them into fists. "Press them hard against your eyes," she said, "and tell me what you see."

It took only a few seconds before I saw white flashes.

"A blind person sees the same thing. Even the totally blind. And so they want to do it all the time. It only takes a few years before the eyes are ruined and have to be removed."

Glass eyes, then, I thought.

"Olivia is learning," she said, hopefully. "I don't have to tell her nearly as often as I used to."

The room grew darker, more tranquil. We heard the bell buoy tolling off Edwards Island, something very rare, I told her. "There has to be enough wind and waves on the water to rock the bell, but no wind here to muffle the sound."

In the candlelight I held her in my arms and asked her to try to go back in her mind to her earliest memory. "It has to be something you never saw in a photograph," I said, "because once you've seen a picture of something, you can't be sure you're really remembering."

"I can't," she said. "I don't have a good memory."

"Everyone says that. Try. You have to try."

"What about you?"

"My first memory is in my father's truck. He had stopped to buy a gallon of apple cider, and then he left me alone in the truck with it. I don't know how long he was gone, but I opened the cap and the cider spilled all over the seat. I remember the sound it made pouring out. That's my very first memory."

"You're sure?"

"I am. What about you?"

"I don't know."

"Close your eyes and think back. Go on. Each time you come up with something, push past it."

"I remember our family doctor sitting on my bed and telling me that I had the measles. I would have been five or six I guess."

"Farther," I said. "Back farther."

"I remember standing in the fog on the first day of school. We couldn't see the bus coming up the hill."

"I was there," I said.

"No, sir."

"Yes, ma'am," I teased her. "I was there beside you. I've always been there."

"Okay then, what kind of shoes was I wearing?"

"Red boots," I joked. "You've always loved red puddle boots. Your grandfather manufactured them and made you rich."

She kissed my lips. "Wrong," she said. "I wore my shiny shoes. I loved them. My mother says I always called my patent leather shoes my shiny shoes."

I propped myself up on my elbow and looked into her eyes. "I remember those shoes," I said.

"Of course you do," she said, "you were there beside me like you said."

"The shoes had elastic straps that held them on. The right strap was loose and the shoe kept falling off."

I told her this with a straight face and an even voice, looking right into her eyes. The way you would tell some-one you love them. She responded at once, taking hold of my wrist to pull herself up in the bed. "You couldn't know that, Terry," she said, emphatically. "Tell me how you knew that."

"I didn't know," I lied. "I was just making it up."

She stared at me a moment before she told me anything more.

"I had sprained my ankle," she said. "I remember it was Halloween. There was a party and we played musical chairs. I tripped and hurt my ankle. For weeks I had to wear a thick bandage wrapped around my foot. It stretched the elastic on my shoe."

She paused and frowned at me. "And you couldn't have known this."

In the morning, I thought. In the morning I will tell you everything.

"No," I said as I gently pulled her close. "I was only guessing."

Sometime in the night I awoke beside her and saw the star-lit sky on her face. A band of moonlight lay across the foot of the bed. This is who I am, I thought. My life is here now beside this woman, and I am a man who will ask nothing for myself except that she never leave me. I gazed at her face on the pillow, her dark hair. I wondered if, in her sleep, she lived somewhere else far from here. I longed to see her waking, for that is when we truly know who a person is, in those first seconds as they are returning from sleep, before they remember where they are in the universe. I made a pledge to the hot coals burning in the stone fireplace and to the white stars beyond the frosted windows, a pledge that I would never leave her, that nothing in the wide world would take me from her side. Her denim dress folded on the chair across the room, her red boots by the door, meant the end of a deep longing inside me.

Sometimes we ask what it is we have done wrong in our lives to deserve heartache and despair. I was already asking this when I awoke in the morning and heard a man speaking to Katherine in the kitchen below me. Her scent was on the pillow next to me, but I was back in LA, in my office. I had to be there because the voice I heard downstairs belonged to Billings.

I walked to the top of the stairs. "I've been on the phone ever since Terry told me the story of you and your father," Billings was saying. "We'll make a gorgeous movie, you can trust us. And are you the father?"

I heard Lawrence answer, "No."

"And to think," Billings went on, "that your father killed that woman and her baby, and all these years he blamed himself, when it was just an accident."

I came down the stairs so fast that I was falling forward when I reached the kitchen. The first thing I saw was the bitter disappointment in Katherine's eyes. It was not unlike the way my father used to look at me.

"Wait," I said. I turned to Lawrence. "I can explain

this," I said. Even as I began I was thinking that I could talk my way out of this. I could take care of this.

It hadn't hit Billings yet. He called to me. "Man, what a trip to get here. I was just telling Katherine about Sara Burke, how perfect she'll be playing her."

"Wait," I said. I raised my hand for him to stop and I turned back to Katherine. "There's no movie," I said. "Nothing like that, Katherine. It's just a misunderstanding."

"No movie?" she said quietly. "Is there a father? Or did you make that up?"

"I didn't make any of it up," I said.

"And the mother and baby?"

"No, I'm saying—"

"*What* are you saying?"

"I care about you."

"You care about me? And the truth? When were you going to tell me the truth?" She turned her back to me, sweeping Olivia up in her arms as she walked away.

"Please," I called to her. But she kept going.

Lobster traps wash ashore on the beaches in Maine. Mostly they are the new type of trap made of wire, but occasionally you will find one of the old traps made of oak slats and fastened with bronze nails that give off a marvelous green flame when they're burned. When I was a boy my father would bring home the wooden traps that had washed ashore at Rose Point and we would burn them in our fireplace and watch the amazing shade of green in the flames. My mother never tired of this, and I have the memory of being very small, sitting on her lap while we watched the fire, and seeing the green flames reflected in her glasses.

Billings and I dragged two traps back to my father's shop. I sawed them into pieces that we burned slowly in the woodstove. I kept thinking that I should walk back to *Serenity* to plead my case. I rehearsed what I might say, going over and over it in my mind. But then there was the memory of Katherine's face, the disappointment in her eyes. And the wrenching in my stomach. The picture of myself as an outsider here once again, as I had always been.

Billings was sitting as close to the woodstove as he

could get without setting himself on fire. He was petting the rabbit, whose dark eyes seemed focused on me. I remembered that it was Christmas Eve, and tonight I was going to carry the rabbit to the cottage for Lawrence.

"You're in love with her, aren't you?" he said.

I was on the telephone to the airlines, on hold with a children's choir singing "Frosty the Snowman" in my ear. The wind shuddered against the windows above my father's desk. I felt something opening inside me. A vast open space was pushing through me, and with it a coldness that seemed to be searching for a place to attach itself, to become permanent in me.

"What difference does it make?" I said.

He saw something outside the windows and stood up. "Here comes the limo," he said.

I watched it approach and pass the shop. I opened the door and stood in the threshold with the sea wind on my face. "Maybe I'll buy a pet rabbit when I get home," I heard Billings say. Then I ran down the porch stairs. I turned onto the lane and ran as hard as I could toward the red taillights out ahead of me, with the feeling that if I didn't stop them I would never see Katherine again.

Lawrence must have seen me behind him in his mirror. He slowed the limousine and waited for me to reach them. I stood at the rear window, and when it opened and I saw Katherine's face, pale and expressionless. "Your shoes," I said, helplessly. "One of your shoes was falling off."

I saw her turn to me, but still her face bore no expression. Olivia moved closer to her, in the direction of my voice.

"I would have told you," I said. "I should have."

I watched her close her eyes and turn her face away. I lingered there for only a moment, looking at the empty space beside her where I had been welcomed once, but where I no longer had a right to be. It made me want to run as far from here as I could go.

I watched the car before it disappeared beyond the gate. I wondered where they were going, and where I would be when they returned to the point.

I spent much of the day talking to Billings, and finally I couldn't stand the sound of my own voice. At sunset I drove into the city. I passed the towering glass banks, black in the night, and the hospital that stood like a fortress. Then I turned onto State Street. At the top of the hill there was a large apartment building. On the first floor in a big lighted room, elderly people were sitting around a Christmas tree. Taped to the windows were paper cutouts of reindeer and wreaths like small children make with blunted scissors.

At the bottom of the hill I saw Callie standing on the corner. She wore her yellow scarf. I told her everything that had happened, and where she could find Charles. I watched her eyes fill with wonder. "You have to see him," I said. "Warren will help you."

"I don't know what to say," she said. "And you're going—"

"Where I belong," I said.

She put her hands on my arms and pulled me close to her. I looked up into the empty blue sky. "I've always thought I should have told Charles something a long time ago," she said. "Something about love. He told me so many times that he didn't deserve to be loved. I should have told him that no one *deserves* to be loved. Love is a gift."

She let go of my arms and began to cry.

44

On the plane back to the West Coast I told Billings what Callie had said about love.

"Nice," he said, without meaning it. "You know what I was looking forward to most about making this movie? It would be *ours*. I mean, we'd finally get to *make* a movie instead of just sweating over somebody else's."

I had my eyes closed and my head back against the seat.

My mind was sorting through the time I'd spent with Katherine, from the moment I first saw her on the shore with Olivia. Sledding. Dancing with her in my father's shop. Sailing. Our one night together.

I could see her face in each scene, the way her eyes responded to me. What I was already missing about her was the stillness that had enclosed us when we were together. How I could be quiet in her presence. Her voice replacing mine.

"I should have stayed," I said. "I should have tried to say something that would have convinced her."

Billings raised his hand for the stewardess and ordered

us each another drink. "In a movie you would have," he said. He looked at his watch.

"What time is it?" I asked.

"Eight twenty," he said.

Five hours more to LA. Which would make it after one in the morning East Coast time when we arrived. Christmas morning. Katherine and Olivia would be studying.

"I think I'll call in," I said to Billings. I dialed my number at The Company and the first message was from my secretary telling me that she had spent the morning transcribing all 187 of my phone messages.

"A hundred and eighty-seven messages," I said.

"That will kill two hours of this flight," he said.

I listened to them all, wanting only to hear Katherine's voice, and feeling myself becoming the person I needed to be to survive where I was going. The kind of man who had chosen not to bury his father because it would have taken too much time. By the time the plane landed I felt cold and closed off.

And then I remembered Katherine kissing me. Leaning toward me with her eyes lit up. The plane had taxied to a stop, and Billings was standing in the aisle waiting for me. "Go on," I said. "I'll see you later."

"Okay, man," he said.

All the passengers filed out past me. The cockpit door opened and I saw the pilot and copilot getting on their dark blue jackets.

"Is everything all right?" a stewardess said to me.

I looked up at her. I wanted to tell her that everything was so far from all right that I didn't think I could stand up.

Inside the terminal I watched the rain lashing across the big glass windows. That sad old Christmas song by Joni Mitchell was playing: "It's coming on Christmas, they're cutting down trees . . . I wish I had a river I could skate away on." I sat down in an empty gate area and began writing Katherine. I kept writing until I'd said everything to her that was in my heart. I wrote for two hours, trying to make it the kind of letter that she would keep for the rest of her life.

Then I walked a long way to the FedEx terminal and arranged for the letter to be delivered to the *Serenity* cottage before the end of Christmas day.

45

I called for a company car to drive me from the airport.

"Haven't seen you in a while, Mr. McQuinn," the driver said, as we made our way onto the expressway. "Merry Christmas."

"Same to you, Rodney," I said.

"No, sir. I'm Miguel. Rodney's not here any more," he said.

I apologized. "Why aren't you home with your family tonight, Miguel?"

"Because I'm here with you, Mr. McQuinn."

I saw his smile. And then my own face in the rearview mirror with a look that I had never seen before. I wondered if this was the face of a man who was giving up.

We were just a few blocks from my apartment building when it hit me that I didn't want to go home. I wasn't sure why, but I knew that I didn't want to open the door and step inside. "Rodney," I said, "can you take me to The Company instead?"

"It's Miguel, sir, and you look tired. Are you sure you don't want to go home? It's after midnight."

I apologized for getting his name wrong again. "I'm sure," I said.

When he dropped me off he got out and opened my door for me. I stuffed some money in his pocket as he was turning away.

"Oh, no, sir, you don't have to do that."

"Merry Christmas, Miguel," I said, as I walked away.

My secretary had left a printed copy of the transcribed telephone messages on my desk along with a dozen red roses and a note saying they were left over from the Christmas party. I picked up the transcript. It was numbered, 197 pages. I sat down and stared at the telephone until I remembered how I'd felt in my father's shop waiting to find out who had left the work order for *Serenity* cottage. Wondering who owned the place after all these years. I had almost given up and left that day.

I finished my drink, then took the elevator down to the basement. I left my shoes outside the squash court, stepped inside the white walls, and started hitting the ball as hard as I could and chasing after it. I kept count of how many times I could hit the ball without it getting past me. It took me twenty or thirty minutes to run it up to twenty-five shots. I told myself I couldn't leave the court until I'd hit fifty in a row.

By then I was so exhausted that I turned out the lights

and laid down on the hardwood floor. I had just begun to drift off when I heard the sound of someone walking in the hallway outside the dark court.

Before I could move, the lights went on and Rosemary Adams, one of the senior people in The Company ducked her head inside the court.

She screamed before I could say anything.

"I'm sorry, Rosie," I told her. She had a handsome guy with her. They were both dressed all in white.

"What are you doing here, Terry?" she asked. "It's Christmas Eve."

"I just needed some exercise," I said.

"Playing in your suit?" the guy said.

I looked at him a moment. "Rosemary didn't tell you that suits are appropriate attire?"

"Don't listen to him," Rosemary said. "Hey, I hear you and Billings have something special cooking?"

I got a sick feeling in my stomach. "Where did you hear that, Rosemary?"

"Fifteen or twenty places."

"It fell through," I told her.

"Too bad," she said. "A father reunited with the daughter he hasn't seen since she was a child? What a story."

"Guess we'll never know," I said.

I wished them both Merry Christmas and left. The door closed behind me. I stood in the hallway a long time, and there wasn't a sound inside the court. Not even voices. I started walking away, and then turned back. I knelt down and looked through the tiny peephole in the door. I could barely make them out. When I saw that they were in each other's arms, I felt sad to the center of my bones.

It was late by the time I got home. Eddie swung the glass door open for me at the apartment building. "Good to see you, Mr. McQuinn. Hey—someone was here to see you a little bit ago," he said.

I wasn't listening, I was thinking about my father. "As long as it wasn't the IRS," I said, as I walked toward the elevator.

"A pretty lady," Eddie called to me.

I turned around and walked straight to him. "Describe her, Eddie. The lady."

He was startled. "Pretty," he said.

"You already said that. What did she look like?"

"Sort of tall, Mr. McQuinn. I'm sorry. Dark hair?"

Before I could stop myself I was interrogating him—holding onto one sleeve of his red jacket. "Dark hair? . . . What else, Eddie?"

It was awful. Eddie had to yell my name before I snapped out of it.

I apologized and went right up to my apartment and microwaved a few things from my freezer. I went back down, trying to be calm. Eddie and I stood outside together while he ate a pepperoni pizza, four croissants, and an apple turnover. I scanned the sidewalk and watched each car that passed.

He kept apologizing. "I see so many people in a day come and go, I'm sorry, I don't remember her too much," he said.

"Don't be silly. It was my fault. I want to ask you something, Eddie," I said.

"Yes, sir."

"I want to know what you think of all this."

He looked confused. "What do you mean, Mr. McQuinn?"

"I mean, what do you think of the way I live."

"Your lifestyle, you mean?"

"That's it, Eddie."

He hesitated, and I thought he wouldn't say anything. "Well, you work too much, I think."

"Everybody in this building works hard don't they?" I asked.

"They do. You're right. But you work harder than the rest."

"Why do you think I do that?"

"Oh, I wouldn't know how to answer that question."

"Come on, Eddie. I've got nobody else I can ask but you. I can't answer the question myself."

Eddie gave me a long look.

"Well, you don't have friends, Mr. McQuinn, I've seen that. That's 'cause you work so much, I think."

I was looking down at his sneakers when he said he had forgotten to tell me that the lady who came to see me had a dog.

Jack, I thought excitedly.

"One of those poodle dogs, special haircut and a little pink sweater."

My heart sank. I knew exactly who it was. Marion Johnson, publisher of one of the local gossip rags. She had been responsible for thirty of my 180 messages while I was away. "Oh, I see," was all I could say.

46

I woke up on Christmas morning and went straight to the office to try and bury myself under work. I was taking a break around noon, calling local movie theaters to find out what was playing, when I saw a woman who looked just like Katherine pause for a moment and look up in my direction before she stepped into a limousine in front of the Wells Fargo bank across the street. I ran out of the office, past my secretary's desk, and across the lobby to the elevator. I pushed the down button and both cars were on the first floor. Instead of waiting, I took the stairs two at a time, and when I burst out into the sunlight I was breathing hard. There were three limousines across the street now. And on my side to the left, two more. And to the right, I counted five in three blocks of traffic backed up all the way to the light. It felt like someone was playing a trick on me.

I started with the three in front of the bank, running from one to the next and knocking on the driver's door, until he opened it and I could peer inside. They were either empty or carrying rap stars I recognized from MTV.

Through those days and the weeks that followed, Billings proved himself a good friend, and I opened up to him, talking honestly to him and concealing nothing, which is the thing one does not do in Hollywood. I told him that it was the way I missed Katherine that made me certain I loved her. How I was already ordering my life around what was absent and most precious to me, waiting for her to ask me to return to her. I did the silly things we all do in such times. I never took a shower without bringing my phone into the bathroom so I could hear it ring. I took my telephone with me even when I skied to the beach in the early mornings. And no matter how discouraged I was at the end of a long day of waiting, I began each day hopeful again that, before dark, my life would change.

Though I was falling down a dark flight of stairs, Billings did his best to hold me up through the winter. One night on the way home from a black-tie premiere, he confronted me.

"You look terrible," he said, as he drove me home.

"No sleep," I said.

"You can get some pills for that."

"You don't understand," I told him. "I don't want to sleep."

He looked at me. In the dashboard light, I saw that the first creases of age had begun to form at the corners of his mouth. I think it was because of this, our shared mortality, that I let him inside my thoughts. I told him that I didn't want to sleep because I kept having the same dream: that when I awoke, Katherine and Olivia would be there.

"If we weren't dreamers," Billings said, "what would we be?"

"Husbands, maybe. Fathers," I said.

We manage, even with our hearts broken. By summer I had moved out of my apartment so I could stop spending time in rooms where all I'd done was wait for the telephone to ring. I got a place off Hazwell Boulevard, paid a decorator to make it look like a men's club, and then I put my head down. What saved me from the loneliness was the work I did to rescue Lewis. You remember he had told me on the telephone when I was at Rose Point that he had failed another audition and was going to take his life. All summer he was in and out of a mental hospital, and on Labor Day morning the police brought him to my apartment after they'd found him walking back and forth across Wilshire Boulevard trying to step into the path of oncoming cars.

I made him take a shower, then I sat him on my couch. He wore my monogrammed bathrobe and my velvet slippers, and despite the situation I had to keep myself from smiling at the sight of him.

"If you hadn't been here, Terry," he said, "I don't know what I would have done."

"When's the last time you ate, Lewis?"

"I don't know. I'm not hungry. I'm too sick to eat."

"I know, but you have to eat. We all do, sick or not. So I'm going to call out for something. What do you want, Mexican or Chinese?"

"Have you tried the Indian place on Stillwater?" he said, perking up. "I don't think Indians close for Labor Day; it should be open."

I called. The place was open. "We ought to get dressed and go out, I think. Don't you?"

Before I took Lewis home I swore that I would turn the city upside down if that's what it took to find him work. And the next day I began a blitzkreig of phone calls, emails, and faxes that lasted right through the autumn.

Nothing happened. And then, just before Thanksgiving, I heard that Max was about to sign a lucrative TV deal for a miniseries. I called him right away. "I have to see you, Max," I said.

"No time until next week," he said.

"I'll be there in fifteen minutes, Max," I said.

He had recently been on a weekend date in Scotland, and immediately upon his return had replaced all three of his personal receptionists with Scottish women who were just beginning to learn to devote themselves to guarding his privacy in a corner office, where on a good day you could see the city through the smog.

He poured us each a scotch on ice, then took a seat behind a desk as big as a billiards table.

"Why don't you go through your Rolodex and throw out all your clients who are older than forty-nine?" he said to me.

"Sounds a little cruel, Max, don't you think?"

"That's how you got where you're at, isn't it?" he said, as he set up the cribbage board and cut a deck of cards to see who dealt first.

"If I'm not mistaken," he said, "you took twenty bucks from me the last time we played."

"Forty," I told him.

"Double or nothing?" he said.

"Fine by me."

While he dealt the cards I told him that Lewis belonged in the lead for his miniseries. "I had a vision about it."

"A vision, hunh? I could name you a few dozen visions that ended up costing me big time in this town. *You* could name some, too, McQuinn."

I kept hoping for bad cards so that the game might soften him up a little, but each of my hands was better than the last, and I beat him in record time.

"You've got that damned Irish luck," he said. "I've got a dartboard coming from Scotland. A beautiful thing. You throw darts?"

"Never," I lied.

"Good," he said. "The dartboard should be here by the end of the week. We'll have a go at it."

In the end Max came through for me. The audition was at the old Meridian theater, and I drove Lewis there myself. "I'll wait for you," I said, as I pulled into a guest slot on the parking lot.

"You might as well keep the car running, Terry," he said.

He got out and began walking toward the door. "Lewis," I called to him. He stopped and looked back. "Break a leg."

He got the part, and that evening I took him to a nice place to celebrate. "I'll never forget this," he said. There were tears in his eyes.

"Yes, you will," I told him. "You'll go on to great, stunning successes that will make this look like small potatoes. But now you have to do something for me, Lewis," I said.

"Name it," he said.

I asked him to ride with me to a beach in Santa Monica. He stood beside me while I scattered my father's ashes into the dark sea. For some reason I had not wanted to do this alone. When we got back in the car Bob Dylan was on the radio singing "Forever Young." We listened until the song was over before we left.

On the way home, we were stopped at a red light next

to a gas station, where a couple of guys were unloading Christmas trees from a flatbed truck and lining them in rows across the parking lot. I was stunned. "I had no idea it was even close to Christmas," I said to Lewis.

"I'm going to buy you a new car with my first pay check," he said.

"I don't want a car," I said, distractedly. "Just tell me how it can be Christmas again."

"What do you mean?" he asked.

"Another year gone? I don't want a car. I want time, Lewis. What am I doing with my life?"

"Helping poor slobs like me."

Suddenly I felt the wait was over. "Look, I've got to drop you off and get home. I've got some calls to make."

I paced around the apartment with the phone in my hand, then I watched some of a Lakers game while I rehearsed what I was going to say to her. Each time a TV commercial came on I hit the mute button and began to dial Katherine's number. Then I stopped. Finally, when the game was over, I placed the call. The phone rang and rang. No answering machine. Nothing. I kept trying all night long, and by morning I was desperately afraid that she and Olivia had disappeared into the wide world and I would never see them again.

Finally, I called Warren.

"Thought I would have heard from you long before now," he said.

"I'll tell you the truth, Warren. I've wanted to call you every day since I left Maine, but I was afraid once I started, I wouldn't be able to stop. I would have called you every day just to see . . . Just to try . . . So, I've been trying to forget, instead," I said. "And I was doing okay until I saw these Christmas trees yesterday"

He listened to me while I told him that I wasn't sure about anything anymore and my heart was still broken.

"Well," he said, "I'm glad you called. I should have called you to thank you."

"For what?"

"Listen, Terry," he went on. "What you did here . . . it worked. I have my brother back, thanks to you. And Charles has his daughter. It's not perfect, but it's so much more than we had before. You gave us all a chance."

I felt grateful for this. I thanked him and told him I had tried to call Katherine in New York.

"They're in South Carolina for the winter," he explained. "I can give you the number there."

"Is Charles there?"

"Yes. Callie's there too."

I closed my eyes and pictured their faces. I didn't have what I wanted most, but this was something I could hold on to. It was a miracle, really.

Warren told me he had taken over for my father at Rose

Point. "I have *Serenity* cottage all wrapped up for winter," he said.

"That's good," I said.

"And the picture of your mother is right where you left it," he said.

I thanked him for that and told him I'd call again, someday soon.

48

As Christmas drew near I surrendered to Billings's plan to spend a week in the Swiss Alps skiing. My heart wasn't in it, but I felt like I owed it to him to at least try. "The mountains," he said. "Once you're up there in those mountains, you'll feel better."

We were scheduled to fly out of LA on the morning of Christmas Eve. The day before I was packing, when I came across the invoice from the Christmas tree farm in Waterville where my father had ordered the tree for *Serenity* before he died. I threw it into the wastebasket and then I picked it up and held it in my hand, recalling the kid who had delivered the tree, how he had dropped out of college to help his father run the business.

On a whim I picked up the phone. Moments later I got the father on the line and asked him if he could take a tree out to the cottage.

"You know there's no one out there this time of year," he said.

"It's something my father did," I said to him. "I know

it's late, but I just realized that it's something I want to do, not just this year but every Christmas from now on."

We talked for a few minutes. I told him he would have to walk in from the gate. I asked him if he could make a stand for the tree and set it on the front porch.

"I know it sounds crazy," I said "but if you can do it, I'll be grateful. I'll pay you whatever you think is fair."

"Don't worry about it," he said. "We're pretty busy here, but if I can get to it, I will. Give me your number and I'll call you back one way or the other."

He called the next morning as Billings and I were checking in our luggage at the airport. "I took the tree out to the house," he said, "but I was a little embarrassed barging in, you know. You didn't tell me anyone would be there."

"Who was there?" I asked quickly.

"A whole family," he said. "An old man was skating on a homemade rink with a little girl. He helped me carry the tree up to the widow's walk. Does a hundred dollars sound okay to you?"

I could barely speak. I spun around to Billings, but his face suggested he already knew what I was going to say. "I've got to see her," I told him.

"I'll call you before the end of the day to make sure you're all right," he replied.

I stood for another beat, frozen.

"Go," he said.

❧

From Boston I caught a commuter to Maine. When we descended through thick storm clouds the plane bounced up and down and the door to the cockpit flew open. The pilot glanced back at us, then apologized for the turbulence. *Just get me there,* I thought.

At the airport in Portland I got into a station wagon with a cardboard "taxi" sign taped to the rear window. Inside I saw that it had been made from a box of Cheerios.

"Do you know how to get to Rose Point?" I asked the driver.

"No one there in the winter," he said.

"I know," I said.

I leaned against the side window and watched bright sunlight break through the clouds, rehearsing what I might say to Katherine. The drive seemed to stretch on for hours.

Finally, the gate was in sight. "Maybe you should wait here for me," I said.

"How long will you be?"

"I don't know."

"It's cold," he said, "if I turn off the engine I might not be able to get it started again."

"Just keep it running," I said.

When I was far enough down Winslow Homer Lane so that I could no longer hear the car's motor, there was nothing but the deep silence that I remembered. Here I am, I thought. I stopped when I saw my father's shop through the trees. I dug through the snow with my hands until I found the coffee can beneath the steps. I opened the door and stepped inside. When I turned, my mother was looking down at me as if she had been expecting me to return.

I was staring into her eyes, trying to hear her voice inside my head, when my phone rang again. I figured Billings must have landed. And what was I going to say to him? *Here I am, waking up after another dream?* I answered the phone.

"Thank you for my Christmas tree, Terry."

It was Olivia. I turned quickly, thinking she was standing behind me.

"Your Christmas tree," I said to her. "I'm glad you like it."

"I know what an elephant looks like now," she said, as though the past year had only been a day.

"You're in the E book?"

"Yes, E for elephant!" she said.

"That's wonderful, Olivia."

"Here's my mommy," she said.

A wave of anxiety washed through me. I walked out of my father's shop, and then when I heard her voice I couldn't move.

"Thank you, Terry," she said. Her voice was so close.

"Merry Christmas," I said.

"We woke you, I'm sorry, I didn't even think about the time difference."

"No, I was awake," I told her. "You made it back to Maine."

"Yes," she said. "We're all here."

"Together," I said. "That's good."

"Terry," she said. "I needed time to think."

"I know," I told her.

"But I was wrong," she said, her voice cracking. "I never should have let you leave."

I started running then and I didn't stop until I saw her in the widow's walk. She was looking out to the sea with her back turned toward me, but Olivia was looking down as if she could see me.

"As soon as we got here, I realized everything," Katherine said.

When she said this, I was in front of the cottage. I realized my shoes were filled with snow. "Katherine," I asked, "are you sure?"

"I'm sure." She hesitated. "But your life is out there, Terry. I know that."

"Not any more," I said. "Turn around, Katherine." I stood there looking up at her until she saw me. In my ear there was the sound of the phone falling as I watched it drop from her hand. Seconds later they burst through the front door and I saw they were both smiling when I took them in my arms.

Their touch that winter morning placed a new sense of wonder in my heart. Since Katherine and I were married I have come to believe that what is common to us all in our varied lives are the things we cannot fully explain. Somehow I think we know this even while we arrange our enterprises with such care, and live on with the illusion that we have everything figured out and all the time left in the world. Our achievements are dazzling, even our failures are often exquisite, but when we look up at the stars at night we cannot say how far the sky goes or where the true god of words and time stands watching over us.

I now live in a father's world, walking Olivia to school, down on my hands and knees hunting for toys lost under the furniture. Counting toes. Changing diapers. There is a tiny statue of Audrey Hepburn, my favorite actress, on the counter by the sink where Olivia helps me give her brother his baths every morning and again at night before bedtime. It's just a little plastic figure that I picked up at some shop on Sunset Boulevard. Now that the baby is teething he grabs hold of the statue and chews on it through his baths. There are his tiny teeth marks on it, and Katherine and I have spoken about how we will carry this with us for the rest of our time together, to remind ourselves how full our lives have been.